THE DAIRYMAN'S DAUGHTER

by

LEGH RICHMOND, M.A.

Grace & Truth Books
Sand Springs, Oklahoma

The Dairyman's Daughter

ISBN 1-58339-126-6

Previously published by
GOSPEL STANDARD BAPTIST TRUST LTD.
FIRST PRINT 1970
RE-PRINTED 1972
SECOND RE-PRINT 1976

Current Printing, Grace & Truth Books, 2005

Cover Design by Ben Gundersen

Grace & Truth Books
3406 Summit Boulevard
Sand Springs, OK 74063
Phone: 918.245.1500
www.graceandtruthbooks.com

Table of Contents

The Dairyman's Daughter

✠❋✠❋✠❋✠❋✠❋✠❋✠❋✠❋✠❋✠❋✠❋✠

BIOGRAPHICAL NOTES OF THE AUTHOR

Date of birth — 29th January 1772.

June 1797 — at age 25 ordained deacon of Brading and Yaverland.

Married — 22nd July 1797 to Mary Chambers, daughter of James William Chambers of Bath.

February 1798 — Ordained priest of Brading and Yaverland.

1805 — appointed to assist the Reverend Fry, Chaplain to the Locke Hospital in London.

30th July 1805 — inducted as Rector of Turvey in Bedfordshire. He was recommended by Mr. Ambrose Serle.

1825 — two of his sons died (he had had a family of ten children).

Beginning of March 1827 — preached his last sermons from Col. iii, 2 and Psalm cxix, 52, 53.

8th May 1827 — died at the age of 55 years, and was buried in Turvey Church.

St. Mary's Church, Brading, where Legh Richmond
was curate with Yaverland Parish Church
from June 1797 to 1805.

Memoir of Legh Richmond, M.A.

Author of the "Dairyman's Daughter" &c.

AMONG those who have contributed to the revival of religion, the subject of the following memoir stands highly distinguished. Few have laboured more earnestly and zealously to promote the growth of piety, both at home and abroad. He has often delighted the public by his eloquence, stimulated it by his zeal, and edified it by his example. The popularity of his literary works has been unexampled. Many at the Last Day, from all parts of the world, who have read his tracts with profit and edification, will rise up and call him blessed.

Legh Richmond was descended from a highly respectable ancestry. His father, Dr. Henry Richmond, was the fifth in lineal male descent from Oliver Richmond, Esq., of Ashton Keynes, in the county of Wilts, on which estate his ancestors had resided from the time of the Conquest. Legh Richmond was born at Liverpool, on the 29th of January, 1772. It was his privilege to have a most pious and estimable mother, endued with a superior understanding, which had been cultivated and improved by an excellent education and much subsequent reading. She anxiously instructed him from his infancy in the Holy Scriptures and in the principles of true religion. She remembered that the child of many prayers is in possession of a richer treasure than the child of the most ample honours and the greatest possessions; for the child of many prayers can never perish, so long as prayer is availing. "I will pour my spirit upon thy seed, and my blessing upon thine offspring (*Isa.* xliv. 3).

But whilst the Lord thus watched over Legh Richmond's infancy, and bestowed so many spiritual blessings that were to bring forth their fruit in due season, the child was not destined to be without his trials and sorrows, to prove, as it were, that this life is but the "pilgrim's journey to a better land." In leaping over a wall, he fell with violence to the ground and injured the left leg so as to contract its growth, and afterwards to impair its use. It was in consequence of this accident that Mr. Richmond received the rudiments of his early education under the sole tuition of his father, who was an excellent classical scholar and well acquainted with literature in general.

When Mr. Richmond was twelve years of age he was placed under the care of Mr. Breach, of Reading, and afterwards under that of Mr. Jones, vicar of Loders and curate of Blandford, in Dorsetshire. In the seventeenth year of his age he was entered at Trinity College, Cambridge, in the month of August, 1789. It was the wish and intention of Mr. Richmond's father that he should follow the profession of the law and be brought to the Bar. In a letter to his father, in which he stated that the Church and the law were the two subjects to which he had directed his attention, he decided in favour of the former as the profession better calculated to promote his own welfare and that of others. "The sacred profession," writes he, "is in itself without doubt the most respectable and the most useful in which any man of principle and education can possibly be engaged." His father reluctantly consented to this view, and Mr. Richmond was ordained deacon in the month of June, 1797.

He proceeded to the degree of M.A. the beginning of July in the same year. On the 22nd of the same month he was married to Mary, only daughter of James William Chambers, Esq., of Bath; immediately after which he proceeded to the Isle of Wight, and entered on the curacies of the parishes of Brading and Yaverland.

After he had resided at Brading about two years, a most important revolution took place in his views and sentiments. He was requested by a college friend to peruse Mr. Wilberforce's "Practical Christianity." A night was spent by him in reading and reflecting upon the important truths contained in this valuable and impressive work. His soul was penetrated to its innermost recesses, and from this period there arose in his mind a solemn consciousness that, however outwardly moral and apparently irreproachable his conduct might appear to men, yet within there was wanting that entire surrender of the heart, that ascendancy of God in the soul, and that devotedness of life and conduct which distinguishes morality from holiness. He felt a conviction of his own state as a guilty and condemned sinner, and under this conviction he sought mercy at the cross of the Saviour. The impressions awakened were followed by a transfer of his time, talents, and affections to the service of his God and his Saviour, and to the spiritual welfare of the flock committed to his care. The Bible became the object of his examination, prayer, and meditation. His aim was to explore truth at its fountain-head, or in the emphatic language of Scripture to "draw water out of the wells of salvation" (*Isa.* xii. 3).

During Mr. Richmond's residence in the Isle of Wight he wrote the tracts which, when collected together, have been so well known as "Annals of the Poor." The first that appeared was "The Dairyman's Daughter;" "The Negro Servant" and "Young Cottager" followed. "The Dairyman's Daughter" rapidly acquired unexampled celebrity. It was extensively read, and many editions of it were rapidly sold, and it became the most popular tract of the time. It was immediately translated, by the Religious Tract Society, into the French and Italian languages. The tract was subsequently translated by the society into most of the continental languages, and it has also obtained a wide circulation in America. It was translated by the Princess Sophia Metstchersky into Russian. A copy of the "Annals of the Poor" was presented by Mr. Richmond to the Emperor of Russia, for which he was kindly thanked by his Imperial Majesty, who sent him in return a ring of considerable value.

Not long after the publication of "The Dairyman's Daughter," the copies circulated in the English language are supposed to have been between one and two millions. It has found its way to the palaces of kings, and has been seen in the hut of the North American Indians. Its author was informed of thirty instances in which it was acknowledged to be instrumental to the conversion of its readers. Two days before Mr. Richmond's death he received a letter mentioning the conversion of two persons (one of whom was a clergyman) by the perusal of his tract "The Dairyman's Daughter." When the letter was given him, he seemed too feeble to open it himself, and desired his son Henry to read it to him. The contents deeply interested him. He raised himself in his chair, lifted up his hand, and then let it fall down again, while he repeatedly shook his head. His manner spoke the greatest humility, as if he would say, "How unworthy of such honour!" For a few moments it seemed to administer a cordial to his fainting spirit, and led the minds of those present to contemplate the near fulfilment of that promise, "They that turn many to righteousness shall shine as the stars for ever and ever."

After a residence of about seven years in the Isle of Wight, in which his labours were so signally blessed, Mr. Richmond moved to London to take a share in the duties of the Lock Chapel. Scarcely was he settled here when he again removed, in 1805, to the rectory of Turvey, in Bedfordshire. In 1814, he was appointed chaplain to the late Duke of Kent, the father of Queen Victoria, and was honoured by many marks of his Royal Highness's esteem and regard.

In 1825, Mr. Richmond's happiness sustained a severe blow by the death of his eldest son, who, after a long absence, died on his voyage from India to England. From this time his health failed, and without any apparent disease, he seemed to be gradually passing away. His daughter thus speaks of his state at this period: "He had a great dislike to keep his bed; and I cannot but acknowledge the goodness of God that it was not necessary. He rose every day to the last, and sat as usual in his study; only getting up a little later, and going to bed earlier, as his strength gradually failed him. The last fortnight he was very silent, and appeared constantly in prayer and meditation, waiting his dismissal and the end of his earthly pilgrimage. At this time, nothing seemed to disturb him, and he appeared to realise the full import of that blessed promise, 'Thou wilt keep him in perfect peace whose mind is stayed on Thee.'" The last Sunday on which Mr. Richmond appeared in the pulpit he preached in the morning from Col. iii. 2, and in the afternoon from Psalm cxix. 52,53. These sermons were particularly solemn. A person going out of church remarked, "This sounds as if it came from the lips of a dying man." From this time the disease visibly increased, and he died on the 8th of May, 1827, aged 55.

A monument has been erected to his memory in the parish church of Turvey, bearing the following inscription:

"Sacred to the memory of the Rev. Legh Richmond, M.A., twenty-two years rector of this parish. Endowed with superior talents, his highest aim was to consecrate them to the service of his God, and to hallow the attainments of the scholar by devoting them to the glory of his Lord and Master. To amiableness of disposition and simplicity of character he united fervency of zeal and holiness of life; eminently blending the charities of earth with the graces of heaven. He preached with fidelity the grace of God in Christ Jesus, and exemplified and adorned by his practice the doctrine which he taught. After many years of unwearied exertion and extensive usefulness, he died with a hope full of immortality, May 8, 1827, aged 55 years, leaving a widow and eight surviving children to mourn the irreparable loss of an affectionate relative; the parish, that of a faithful and endeared pastor; and the Church of God, the too early removal of one of its brightest ornaments."

PART I.

HOW THE DAIRYMAN'S DAUGHTER
INTRODUCED HERSELF

IT IS a delightful employment to discover and trace the operations of divine grace as they are manifested in the dispositions and lives of God's real children. It is peculiarly gratifying to observe how frequently, among the poorer classes of mankind, the sunshine of mercy beams upon the heart, and bears witness to the image of Christ which the Spirit of God has impressed thereupon. Among such, the sincerity and simplicity of the Christian character appear unencumbered by those obstacles to spirituality of mind and conversation which too often prove a great hindrance to those who live in the higher ranks. Many are the difficulties which riches, worldly consequence, high connections, and the luxuriant refinements of polished society throw in the way of religious profession. Happy indeed it is (and some such happy instances I know) where grace has so strikingly supported its conflict with natural pride, self-importance, the allurements of luxury, ease, and worldly opinion, that the noble and mighty appear adorned with genuine poverty of spirit, self-denial, humble-mindedness, and deep spirituality of heart.

But in general, if we want to see religion in its most simple and pure character, we must look for it among the poor of this world who are rich in faith. How often is the poor man's cottage the palace of God! Many can truly declare that they have there learned the most valuable lessons of faith and hope, and there witnessed the most

1

striking demonstrations of the wisdom, power, and goodness of God.

The character which the present narrative is designed to introduce to the notice of my readers is given *from real life and circumstances*. I first became acquainted with her by receiving the following letter, which I transcribe from the original now before me: —

'REV. SIR,

'I take the liberty to write to you. Pray excuse me, for I have never spoken to you. But I once heard you when you preached at —— Church. I believe you are a faithful preacher to warn sinners to flee from the wrath that will be revealed against all those that live in sin and die impenitent. Pray go on in the strength of the Lord. And may He bless you, and crown your labour of love with success, and give you souls for your hire!

'The Lord has promised to be with those whom He calls and sends forth to preach His word, to the end of time, for without Him we can do nothing. I was much rejoiced to hear of those marks of love and affection to that poor soldier of the S.D. Militia. Surely the love of Christ sent you to that poor man: may that love ever dwell richly in you by faith! May it constrain you to seek the wandering souls of men with the fervent desire to spend and be spent for His glory! May the unction of the Holy Spirit attend the word spoken by you with power, and convey deep conviction to the hearts of your hearers! May many of them experience the divine change of being made new creatures in Christ!

'Sir, be fervent in prayer with God for the conversion of sinners. His power is great, and who can withstand it? He has promised to answer the prayer of faith that is put up in His Son's Name. "Ask what ye will, it shall be granted you." How this should strengthen our

2

faith, when we pray! Oh, that sweet inspiring hope; how it lifts up the fainting spirits, when we look over the precious promises of God! What a mercy if we know Christ and the power of His resurrection in our own hearts! Through faith in Christ we rejoice in hope, and look up in expectation of that time drawing near, when all shall know and fear the Lord, and when a nation shall be born in a day.

'What a happy time, when Christ's kingdom shall come! Then shall "His will be done on earth, as it is in heaven." Men shall be daily fed with the manna of His love, and delight themselves with the Lord all the day long. Then what a paradise below they will enjoy! How it animates and enlivens my soul with vigour to pursue the ways of God, that I may even now bear some humble part in giving glory to God and the Lamb!

'Sir, I began to write this on Sunday, being detained from attending on public worship. My dear and only sister, living as a servant with Mrs —— was so ill, that I came here to attend in her place and on her. But now she is no more.

'I was going to entreat you to write to her in answer to this; she being convinced of the evil of her past life, and that she had not walked in the ways of God, nor sought to please Him. But she earnestly desired to do so. This makes me have a comfortable hope that she is gone to glory, and that she is now joining in sweet concert with the angelic host in heaven to sing the wonders of redeeming love. I hope I may now write, "Blessed are the dead which die in the Lord."

'She expressed a desire to receive the Lord's Supper, and commemorate His precious death and sufferings. I told her, as well as I was able, what it was to receive Christ into her heart: but as her weakness of body increased, she did not mention it again. She seemed quite resigned before she died. I do hope she is gone from a world of death and sin to be with God for ever.

'Sir, I hope you will not be offended with me, a poor ignorant person, to take such a liberty as to write to you. But I trust, as you are called to instruct sinners in the ways of God, you will bear with me, and be so kind to answer this ill-written letter, and give me some instruction. It is my heart's desire to have the mind that was in Christ, that when I awake up in His likeness then I may be satisfied.

'My sister expressed a wish that you might bury her. The minister of our parish, whither she will be carried, cannot come. She will lie at ———. She died on Tuesday morning, and will be buried on Friday or Saturday (whichever is most convenient to you) at three o'clock in the afternoon. Please to send an answer by the bearer, to let me know whether you can comply with this request.

'From your unworthy servant,
ELIZABETH W———.'

I was much struck with the simple and earnest strain of devotion which this letter breathed. It was but indifferently written and spelt. But this the rather tended to endear the hitherto unknown writer, as it seemed characteristic of the union of humbleness of station with eminence of piety. I felt quite thankful that I was favoured with a correspondent of this description; the more so, as such characters were at that time very rare in the neighbourhood. I have often wished that epistolary intercourse of this kind were more encouraged and practised among us. I have the greatest reason to speak well of its effect both on myself and others. Communication by letter as well as by conversation with the pious poor, has often been the instrument of animating and reviving my own heart in the midst of my duty, and of giving me the most profitable information for the general conduct of the ministerial office.

As soon as the letter was read, I inquired who was the bearer of it.

'He is waiting at the outside of the gate, Sir,' was the reply.

I went out to speak to him, and saw a venerable old man, whose long hoary hair and deeply wrinkled countenance commanded more than common respect. He was resting his arm upon the gate, and tears were streaming down his cheeks. On my approach he made a low bow, and said—

'Sir, I have brought you a letter from my daughter; but I fear you will think us very bold in asking you to take so much trouble.'

'By no means,' I replied; 'I shall be truly glad to oblige you and any of your family in this matter, provided it be quite agreeable to the minister of your parish.'

'Sir, he told me yesterday, that he should be very glad if I could procure some gentleman to come and bury my poor child for him, as he lives five miles off, and has particular business on that day; so when I told my daughter, she asked me to come to you, Sir, and bring that letter, which would explain the matter.'

I desired him to come into the house, and then said, 'What is your occupation?'

'Sir, I have lived most of my days in a little cottage at ——, six miles from here. I have rented a few acres of ground, and kept some cows, which, in addition to my day-labor, has been the means of supporting and bringing up my family.'

'What family have you?'

'A wife now getting very aged and helpless, two sons, and one daughter; for my other poor dear child is just departed out of this wicked world.'

'I hope for a better.'

'I hope so too; poor thing, she did not use to take to such good ways as her sister; but I do believe that her sister's manner of talking with her before she died was the means of saving her soul. What a mercy it is to have such a child as mine is! I never thought about my own soul seriously till she, poor girl, begged me to flee from the wrath to come.'

'How old are you?'

'Nearly seventy, and my wife is older; we are getting old and almost past our labour, but our daughter has left a good place, where she lived in service, on purpose to come home and take care of us and our little dairy. And a dear, dutiful, affectionate girl she is.'

'Was she always so?'

'No, Sir; when she was very young, she was all for the world, and pleasure, and dress, and company. Indeed, we were all very ignorant, and thought if we took care for this life, and wronged nobody, we should be sure to go to heaven at last. My daughters were both wilful, and like ourselves, strangers to the ways of God and the word of His grace. But the eldest of them went out to service, and some years ago she heard a sermon preached at —— Church by a gentleman that was going to ——, as chaplain to the colony, and from that time she seemed quite another creature. She began to read the Bible, and became sober and steady. The first time she returned home afterwards to see us, she brought us a guinea which she had saved from her wages, and said as we were getting old, she was sure we should want help; adding, that she did not wish to spend it in fine clothes, as she used to do, only to feed pride and vanity. She said she would rather show gratitude to her dear father and mother, because Christ had shown such mercy to her.

'We wondered to hear her talk, and took great delight in her company; for her temper and behaviour were so humble and kind, she seemed so desirous to do us good both in soul and body, and was so different from what we had ever seen her before, that, careless and ignorant as we had been, we began to think there must be something real in religion, or it never could alter a person so much in a little time.

'Her youngest sister, poor soul! used to laugh and ridicule her at that time, and said her head was turned with her new ways. "No, sister," she would say, "not my head, but I hope my heart is turned from the love of sin to the love of God. I wish you may one day see, as I do, the danger and vanity of your present condition." 'Her poor sister would reply, "I do not want to hear any of your preaching; I am no worse than other people, and that is enough for me." "Well, sister," Elizabeth would say, "if you will not hear me, you cannot hinder me from praying for you, which I do with all my heart."

'And now, Sir, I believe those prayers are answered. For when her sister was taken ill, Elizabeth went to Mrs ——'s to wait in her place, and take care of her. She said a great deal to her about her soul, and the poor girl began to be so deeply affected, and sensible of her past sin, and so thankful for her sister's kind behaviour, that it gave her great hopes indeed for her sake. When my wife and I went to see her as she lay sick, she told us how grieved and ashamed she was of her past life; but said, she had a hope through grace that her dear sister's Saviour would be her Saviour too; for she saw her own sinfulness, felt her own helplessness, and only wished to cast herself upon Christ as her hope and salvation.

'And now, Sir, she is gone, and I hope and think her sister's prayers for her conversion to God have been answered. The Lord grant the same for her poor father and mother's sake likewise!'

This conversation was a very pleasing commentary upon the letter which I had received, and made me anxious both to comply with the request, and to become acquainted with the writer. I promised the good dairyman to attend on the Friday at the appointed hour; and after some more conversation respecting his own state of mind under the present trial, he went away.

He was a reverend old man; his furrowed cheeks, white locks, weeping eyes, bent shoulders, and feeble gait, were characteristic of the aged pilgrim. As he slowly walked onward, supported by a stick, which seemed to have been the companion of many a long year, a train of reflections occurred, which I retrace with pleasure and emotion.

At the appointed hour I arrived at the church; and, after a little while, was summoned to the churchyard gate to meet the funeral procession. The aged parents, the elder brother, and the sister, with other relatives, formed an affectionate group. I was struck with the humble, pious and pleasing countenance of the young woman from whom I had received the letter. It bore the marks of great seriousness without affectation, and of much serenity mingled with a glow of devotion.

A circumstance occurred during the reading of the Burial Service, which I think it right to mention, as one among many testimonies of the solemn and impressive tendency of our truly evangelical Liturgy.

A man of the village, who had hitherto been of a very careless and even profligate character, went into the church through mere curiosity, and with no better purpose than that of vacantly gazing at the ceremony. He came likewise to the grave, and during the reading of those prayers which are appointed for that part of the service, his mind received a deep, serious conviction of his sin and spiritual danger. It was an impression that never wore off, but gradually ripened into the most satisfactory evidence of an entire change, of which I had many and long-continued proofs. He always referred to the Burial Service, and to some particular sentences of it, as the clearly ascertained instrument of bringing him, through grace, to the knowledge of the truth.

The day was therefore one to be remembered. Remembered let it be by those who love to hear 'the short and simple annals of the poor.'

Was there not a manifest and happy connection between the circumstances that providentially brought the serious and the careless to the same grave on that day together? How much do they lose who neglect to trace the leadings of God in providence, as links in the chain of His eternal purpose of redemption and grace!

'While infidels may scoff, let us adore!'

After the service was concluded, I had a short conversation with the good old couple and their daughter. She told me that she intended to remain a week or two at the gentleman's house where her sister died, till another servant should arrive and take her sister's place.

'I shall be truly obliged,' said she, 'by an opportunity of conversing with you, either there or at my father's when I return home, which will be in the course of a fortnight at the furthest. I shall be glad to talk to you about my sister, whom you have just buried.'

Her aspect and address were highly interesting. I promised to see her very soon; and then returned home, quietly reflecting on the circumstances of the funeral at which I had been engaged. I blessed the God of the poor, and prayed that the poor might become rich in faith, and the rich be made poor in spirit.

PART II.

A NEW FRIENDSHIP MAKES GOOD PROGRESS

A SWEET solemnity often possesses the mind, whilst retracing past intercourse with departed friends. How much is this increased, when they were such as lived and died in the Lord! The remembrance of former scenes and conversations with those who, we believe, are now enjoying the uninterrupted happiness of a better world, fills the heart with pleasing sadness, and animates the soul with the hopeful anticipation of a day when the glory of the Lord shall be revealed in the assembling of all His children together, never more to be separated. Whether they were rich or poor, while on earth, is a matter of trifling consequence: the valuable part of their character is, that they are 'kings and priests unto God'; and this is their true nobility. In the number of now-departed believers, with whom I once loved to converse on the grace and glory of the kingdom of God, was the dairyman's daughter.

About a week after the funeral, I went to visit the family at ——, in whose service the youngest sister had lived and died, and where Elizabeth was requested to remain for a short time in her stead.

The house was a large and venerable mansion. It stood in a beautiful valley at the foot of a high hill. It was embowered in fine woods, which were interspersed in every direction with rising, falling, and swelling grounds. The manor-house had evidently descended through a long line of ancestry, from a distant period of time. The Gothic character of its original architecture was still preserved in the latticed windows, adorned with carved divisions and pillars of stonework. Several pointed terminations also, in the construction of the roof, according to the custom of our forefathers, fully corresponded with the general features of the building.

One end of the house was entirely clothed with the thick foliage of an immense ivy, which climbed beyond customary limits, and embraced a lofty chimney up to its very summit. Such a tree seemed congenial to the walls that supported it, and conspired with the antique fashion of the place to carry imagination back to the days of our ancestors.

As I approached, I was led to reflect on the lapse of ages, and the successive generations of men, each in their turn occupying lands, houses, and domains; each in their turn also disappearing, and leaving their inheritance to be enjoyed by others. David once observed the same, and cried out, 'Behold. Thou hast made my days as a handbreadth, and mine age is as nothing before Thee; verily every man at his best state is altogether vanity. Surely every man walketh in a vain show; surely they are disquieted in vain; he heapeth up riches, and knoweth not who shall gather them.'

Happy would it be for the rich, if they more frequently meditated on the uncertainty of all their possessions, and the frail nature of every earthly tenure. 'Their inward thought is, that their houses shall continue for ever, and their dwelling-places to all generations; they call their lands after their own names. Nevertheless man being in honour abideth not; he is like the beasts that perish. This their way is their folly; yet their posterity approve their sayings. Like sheep they are laid in the grave; death shall feed on them; and their beauty shall consume in the grave from their dwelling.'

As I advanced to the mansion, a pleasing kind of gloom overspread the front; it was occasioned by the shade of trees, and gave a characteristic effect to the ancient fabric. I instantly recollected that death had very recently visited the house, and that one of its present inhabitants was an affectionate mourner for a departed sister.

There is a solemnity in the thought of a recent death, which will associate itself with the very walls from whence we are conscious that a soul has just taken its flight to eternity.

After passing some time in conversation with the superiors of the family, in the course of which I was much gratified by hearing of the unremitted attention which the elder sister had paid to the younger during the illness of the latter, I received likewise other testimonies of the excellency of her general character and conduct in the house. I then took leave to request permission to see her, agreeably to the promise I had made at the funeral, not many days before.

I was shown into a parlour, where I found her alone. She was in deep mourning. She had a calmness and serenity in her countenance which exceedingly struck me, and impressed some idea of those attainments which a further acquaintance with her afterwards so much increased.

She spoke of her sister. I had the satisfaction of finding that she had given very hopeful proofs of a change of heart before she died. The prayers and earnest exhortations of Elizabeth had been blessed to a happy effect. She described what had passed with such a mixture of sisterly affection, and pious dependence on the mercy of God to sinners, as convinced me that her own heart was under the influence of 'pure and undefiled religion.'

She requested leave occasionally to correspond with me on serious subjects, stating that she needed much instruction. She hoped I would pardon the liberty which she had taken by introducing herself to my notice. She expressed a trust that the Lord would overrule both the death of her sister, and the personal acquaintance with me that resulted from it, to a present and future good, as it respected herself, and also her parents, with whom she statedly lived, and to whom she expected to return in a few days.

Finding that she was wanted in some household duty, I did not remain long with her, but left her with an assurance that I proposed to visit her parents very shortly.

'Sir,' said she, 'I take it very kind that you have condescended to leave the company of the rich, and converse with the poor. I wish I could have said more to you respecting my own state of mind. Perhaps I shall be better able another time. When you next visit me, instead of finding me in these noble walls, you will see me in a poor cottage. But I am happiest when there. Once more, Sir, I thank you for your past kindness to me and mine, and may God in many ways bless you for it!'

I quitted the house with no small degree of satisfaction, in consequence of the new acquaintance which I had formed. I discovered traces of a cultivated as well as a spiritual mind. I felt that religious intercourse with those of low estate may be rendered eminently useful to others, whose outward station and advantages are far above their own.

How often does it appear that 'God hath chosen the weak things of the world to confound the things which are mighty; and base things of the world, and things which are despised, hath God chosen, and things which are not, to bring to nought things that are: that no flesh should glory in His presence!'

It was not unfrequently my custom, when my mind was filled with any interesting subject for meditation, to seek some spot where the beauties of natural prospect might help to form pleasing and useful associations. I therefore ascended gradually to the very summit of the hill adjoining the mansion where my visit had just been made. Here was placed an elevated sea-mark: it was in the form of a triangular pyramid, and built of stone. I sat down on the ground near it, and looked at the surrounding prospect, which was distinguished for beauty and magnificence. It was a lofty station commanding a complete circle of interesting objects to engage the spectator's attention.

Southward the view was terminated by a long range of hills, at about six miles' distance. They met, to the westward, another chain of hills, of which the one whereon I sat formed a link, and the whole together nearly encompassed a rich and fruitful valley, filled with cornfields and pastures. Through this vale winded a small valley for many miles: much cattle were feeding on its banks. Here and there lesser eminences arose in the valley; some covered with wood, others with corn or grass, and a few with heath or fern. One of these little hills was distinguished by a parish church at the top, presenting a striking feature in the landscape. Another of these elevations, situated in the centre of the valley, was adorned with a venerable holly-tree, which has grown there for ages. Its singular height and wide-spreading dimensions not only render it an object of curiosity to the traveler, but of daily usefulness to the pilot, as a mark visible from the sea, whereby to direct his vessel safe into harbour. Villages, churches, country-seats, farmhouses, and cottages, were scattered over every part of the southern valley. In this direction also, at the foot of the hill where I was stationed, appeared the ancient mansion which I had just quitted, embellished with its woods, groves, and gardens.

South-eastward, I saw the open ocean, bounded only by the horizon. The sun shone, and gilded the waves with a glittering light that sparkled in the most brilliant manner. More to the east, in continuation of that line of hills where I was placed, rose two downs, one beyond the other; both covered with sheep, and the sea just visible over the farthest of them, as a terminating boundary. In this point ships were seen, some sailing, others at anchor. Here the little river, which watered the southern valley, finished its course, and ran through meadows into the sea, in an eastward direction.

On the north the sea appeared like a noble river, varying from three to seven miles in breadth, between the banks of the opposite coast and those of the island which I inhabited. Immediately underneath me was a fine woody district of country, diversified by many pleasing objects. Distant towns were visible on the opposite shore. Numbers of ships occupied the sheltered station which this northern channel afforded them. The eye roamed with delight over an expanse of near and remote beauties, which alternately caught the observation, and which harmonised together, and produced a scene of peculiar interest.

Westward the hills followed each other, forming several intermediate and partial valleys, in a kind of undulations, like the waves of the sea; and bending to the south, completed the boundary of the larger valley before described, to the south-ward of the hill on which I sat. In many instances the hills were cultivated with corn to their very summits, and seemed to defy the inclemency of the weather, which, at these heights, usually renders the ground incapable of bringing forth and ripening the crops of grain. One hill alone, the highest in elevation and about ten miles to the south-westward, was enveloped in a cloud, which just permitted a dim and hazy sight of a signal-post, a lighthouse, and an ancient chantry, built on its summit.

Amidst these numerous specimens of delightful scenery I found a mount for contemplation, and here I indulged it.

'How much of the natural beauties of Paradise still remain in the world, although its spiritual character has been so awfully defaced by sin! But when divine grace renews the heart of the fallen sinner, Paradise is regained, and much of its beauty restored to the soul. As this prospect is compounded of hill and dale, land and sea, woods and plains, all sweetly blended together, and relieving each other in the landscape, so do the gracious dispositions wrought in the soul produce a beauty and harmony of scene to which it was before a stranger.'

I looked towards the village in the plain below, where the dairyman's younger daughter was buried. I retraced the simple solemnities of the funeral. I connected the principles and conduct of her sister with the present probably happy state of her soul in the world of spirits, and was greatly impressed with a sense of the importance of family influence as a means of grace. 'That young woman,' I thought, 'has been the conductor of not only a sister, but perhaps a father and mother also, to the true knowledge of God, and may, by divine blessing, become so to others. It is a glorious occupation to win souls to Christ, and guide them out of Egyptian bondage through the wilderness into the promised Canaan. Happy are the families who are walking hand in hand together, as pilgrims, towards the heavenly country. May the number of such be daily increased!'

Casting my eye over the numerous dwellings in the vales on my right and left, I could not help thinking, 'How many of their inhabitants are ignorant of the ways of God, and strangers to His grace! May this thought stimulate to activity and diligence in the cause of immortal souls! They are precious in God's sight-they ought to be so in ours.'

Some pointed and affecting observations to that effect recurred to my mind as having been made by the young person with whom I had been just conversing. Her mind appeared to be much impressed with the duty of speaking and acting for God 'while it is day'; conscious that 'the night cometh, when no man can work.' Her laudable anxiety on this head was often testified to me afterwards, both by letter and conversation. What she felt herself, in respect to endeavours to do good, she happily communicated to others with whom she corresponded or conversed.

Time would not permit my continuing so long in the enjoyment of these meditations on this lovely mount of enjoyment, as my heart desired. On my return home I wrote a few lines to the dairyman's daughter, chiefly dictated by the train of thought which had occupied my mind while I sat on the hill. On the next Sunday evening I received her reply, of which the following is a transcript:—

'Sunday.

'REV. SIR,

'I am this day deprived of an opportunity of attending the house of God, to worship Him. But, glory be to His name, He is not confined to time or place. I feel Him present with me where I am, and His presence makes my paradise; for where He is, is heaven. I pray God that a double portion of His grace and Holy Spirit may rest upon you this day; that His blessings may attend all your faithful labours; and that you may find the truth of His words assuring us, that wherever we assemble together in His name, there He is in the midst to bless every waiting soul.

18

'How precious are all His promises! We ought never to doubt the truth of His word. For He will never deceive us if we go on in faith, always expecting to receive what His goodness waits to give.

Dear Sir, I have felt it very consoling to read your kind letter today. I feel thankful to God for ministers in our Church who love and fear His name: there it is where the people in general look for salvation; and there may they ever find it, for Jesus' sake! May His word, spoken by you His chosen vessel of grace, be made spirit and life to their dead souls! May it come from you as an instrument in the hands of God, as sharp arrows from a strong archer, and strike a death-blow to all their sins! How I long to see the arrows of conviction fasten on the minds of those that are hearers of the word, and not doers! O Sir! be ambitious for the glory of God and the salvation of souls. It will add lustre to your crown in glory, as well as to your present joy and peace. We should be willing to spend and be spent in His service, saying, "Lord, may Thy will be done by me on earth, even as it is by the angels in heaven." So you may expect to see His face with joy, and say—"Here am I, Lord, and all the souls Thou hast given me."

'It seems wonderful that we should neglect any opportunity of doing good, when there is, if it be done from love to God and His creatures, a present reward of grace, in reflecting that we are using the talents committed to our care according to the power and ability which we receive from Him. God requires not what He has not promised to give. But when we look back, and reflect that there have been opportunities in which we have neglected to take up our cross and speak and act for God, what a dejection of mind we feel! We are then justly filled with shame. Conscious of being ashamed of Christ, we cannot

19

come with that holy boldness to a throne of grace, nor feel that free access when we make our supplications.

'We are commanded to provoke one another to love and good works; and where two are agreed together in the things of God, they may say—

    ' "And if our fellowship below
      In Jesus is so sweet,
    What heights of rapture shall we know,
      When round the throne we meet!"

'Sir, I hope Mrs —— and you are both of one heart and one mind. Then you will sweetly agree in all things that make for your present and eternal happiness. Christ sent His disciples out, not singly, but two and two, that they might comfort and help each other in those ways and works which their Lord commanded them to pursue.

'It has been my lot to have been alone the greatest part of the time that I have known the ways of God. I therefore find it such a treat to my soul when I can meet with anyone who loves to talk of the goodness and love of God, and all His gracious dealings. What a comfortable reflection, to think of spending a whole eternity in that delightful employment! to tell to listening angels His love "immense, unsearchable!"

'Dear Sir, I thank you for your kindness and condescension in leaving those that are of high rank and birth in the world, to converse with me, who am but a servant here below. But when I consider what a high calling, what honour and dignity, God has conferred upon me, to be called His child, to be born of His Spirit, made an heir of glory, and joint-heir with Christ, how humble and circumspect should I be in all my ways, as a dutiful and loving child to an affectionate and loving Father! When I seriously consider these things, it fills me with love and gratitude to God, and I do not wish for any higher station, nor envy the rich. I rather pity them if they are not good as well as great. My blessed Lord was pleased to appear in the form of a servant; and I long to be like Him.

'I did not feel in so happy a frame of conversation that day, nor yet that liberty to explain my thoughts which I sometimes do. The fault must have been all in myself; for there was nothing in you but what seemed to evidence a Christian spirit, temper, and disposition. I very much wished for an opportunity to converse with you. I feel very thankful to God that you do take up the cross, and despise the shame; if you are found faithful, you will soon sit down with Him in glory.

'I have written to the Rev. Mr ——, to thank him for permitting you to perform the burial service at —— over my dear departed sister, and to tell him of the kind way in which you consented to do it. I should mention that your manner of reading the service on that day had a considerable effect on the hearers.

'Pray excuse all faults, and correct my errors. I expect in a few days to return home to my parents' house. We shall rejoice to see you there.

'From your humble servant in Christ,
'E — W—.'

It was impossible to view such a correspondent with indifference. I had just returned from a little cottage assembly, where, on Sunday evenings, I sometimes went to instruct a few poor families in one of the hamlets belonging to my parish. I read the letter, and closed the day with thanksgiving to God for thus enabling those who fear His name to build up each other in fear and love.

Of old time, 'they that feared the Lord spake often one to another; and the Lord hearkened, and heard it; and a book of remembrance was written before Him for them that feared the Lord, and that thought upon His name.' That book of remembrance is not yet closed.

PART III.

THE SIMPLICITY OF THE DAIRYMAN'S HOME

THE MIND of man is like a moving picture, supplied with objects, not only from contemplation on things present, but from the fruitful sources of recollection and anticipation.

Memory retraces past events, and restores an ideal reality to scenes which are gone by for ever. They live again in revived imagery, and we seem to hear and see with renewed emotions what we heard and saw at a former period. Successions of such recollected circumstances often form a series of welcome memorials. In religious meditations, the memory becomes a sanctified instrument of spiritual improvement.

Another part of this animated picture is furnished by the pencil of Hope. She draws encouraging prospects for the soul, by connecting the past and the present with the future. Seeing the promises afar off, she is persuaded of their truth, and embraces them as her own.

The Spirit of God gives a blessing to both these acts of the mind, and employs them in the service of religion. Every faculty of body and soul, when considered as a part of 'the purchased possession' of the Saviour, assumes a new character. How powerfully does the apostle, on this ground, urge a plea for holy activity and watchfulness! 'What? know ye not that your body is the temple of the Holy Ghost which is in you, which ye have of God? And ye are not your own; for ye are bought with a price: therefore glorify God in your body, and in your spirit, which are God's.'

The Christian may derive much profit and enjoyment from the use of the memory as it concerns those transactions in which he once bore a part. In his endeavours to recall past conversations and intercourse with deceased friends in particular, the powers of remembrance greatly improve by exercise. One revived idea produces another, till the mind is most agreeably and usefully occupied with lively and holy imaginations.

'Lull'd in the countless chambers of the brain,
    Our thoughts are link'd by many a hidden chain;
Awake but one, and lo! what myriads rise!
    Each stamps its image as the other flies;
Each, as the varied avenues of sense
    Delight or sorrow to the soul dispense,
Brightens or fades: yet all, with sacred art,
    Control the latent fibres of the heart.'

May it please God to bless, both to the reader and the writer, this feeble attempt to recollect some of the communications which I once enjoyed in my visits to the Dairyman's dwelling!

Very soon after the receipt of the last letter, I rode for the first time to see the family at their own house. The principal part of the road lay through retired, narrow lanes, beautifully overarched with groves of nut and other trees, which screened the traveller from the rays of the sun, and afforded many interesting objects for admiration in the flowers, shrubs, and young trees which grew upon the high banks on each side of the road. Many grotesque rocks, with little trickling streams of water occasionally breaking out of them, varied the recluse scenery, and produced a romantic and pleasing effect.

Here and there the most distant prospect beyond was observable through gaps and hollow places on the road-side. Lofty hills, with many signal-posts, obelisks, and lighthouses on their summits, appeared at these intervals; rich cornfields were also visible through some of the open places; and now and then, when the road ascended a hill, the sea, with ships at various distances, was seen. But for the most part shady seclusion, and objects of a more minute and confined nature, gave a character to the journey, and invited contemplation.

How much do they lose who are strangers to serious meditation on the wonders and beauties of nature! How gloriously the God of creation shines in His works! Not a tree, or leaf, or flower, not a bird or insect, but it proclaims in glowing language, 'God made me.'

As I approached the village where the good old Dairyman dwelt, I observed him in a little field driving his cows before him towards a yard and hovel which adjoined his cottage. I advanced very near him without his observing me, for his sight was dim. On my calling out to him he started at the sound of my voice, but with much gladness of heart welcomed me, saying—'Bless your heart, Sir, I am glad you are come: we have looked for you every day this week.'

The cottage-door opened, and the daughter came out, followed by her aged and infirm mother. The sight of me naturally brought to recollection the grave at which we had before met. Tears of affection mingled with the smile of satisfaction with which I was received by these worthy cottagers. I dismounted, and was conducted through a neat little garden, part of which was shaded by two large overspreading elm-trees, to the house. Decency and order were manifested within and without. No excuse was made here, on the score of poverty, for confusion and uncleanliness in the disposal of their little household.

Everything wore the aspect of neatness and propriety. On each side of the fireplace stood an old oaken arm-chair, where the venerable parents rested their weary limbs after the day's labour was over. On a shelf in one corner lay two Bibles, with a few religious books and tracts. The little room had two windows; a lovely prospect of hills, woods, and fields appeared through one; and the other was more than half obscured by the branches of a vine which was trained across it; between its leaves the sun shone, and cast a cheerful light over the whole place.

'This,' thought I. 'is a fit residence for piety, peace, and contentment. May I learn a fresh lesson for advancement in each, through the blessing of God on this visit!'

'Sir,' said the daughter, 'we are not worthy that you should come under our roof. We take it very kind that you should travel so far to see us.'

'My Master' I replied, 'came a great deal farther to visit us poor sinners. He left the bosom of His Father, laid aside His glory, and came down to this lower world on a visit of mercy and love; and ought not we, if we profess to follow Him, to bear each other's infirmities, and go about doing good, as He did?'

The old man now entered, and joined his wife and daughter in giving me a cordial welcome. Our conversation soon turned to the loss they had so lately sustained. The pious and sensible disposition of the daughter was peculiarly manifested, as well in what she said to her parents, as in what she more immediately addressed to myself. I had now a further opportunity of remarking the good sense and agreeable manner which accompanied her expressions of devotedness to God, and love to Christ for the great mercies which He had bestowed upon her. During her residence in different gentlemen's families where she had been in service, she had acquired a superior behaviour and address; but sincere piety rendered her very humble and unassuming in manner and conversation. She seemed anxious to improve the opportunity of my visit to the best purpose for her own and her parents' sake; yet there was nothing of unbecoming forwardness, no self-confidence or conceitedness in her conduct. She united the firmness and solicitude of the Christian with the modesty of the female and the dutifulness of the daughter. It was impossible to be in her company, and not observe how truly her temper and conversation adorned the principles which she professed.

I soon discovered how eager and how successful also she had been in her endeavours to bring her father and mother to the knowledge and experience of the truth. This is a lovely feature in the character of a young Christian. If it have pleased God, in the free dispensation of His mercy, to call the child by His grace, while the parent remains still in ignorance and sin, how great is the duty incumbent on that child to do what is possible to promote the conversion of those to whom so much is owing! Happy is it when the ties of grace sanctify those of nature!

The aged couple evidently regarded and spoke of this daughter as their teacher and admonisher in divine things, while at the same time they received from her every token of filial submission and obedience, testified by continual endeavours to serve and assist them to the utmost of her power in the daily concerns of the household.

The religion of this young woman was of a highly spiritual character, and of no ordinary attainment. Her views of the divine plan in saving the sinner were clear and Scriptural. She spoke much of the joys and sorrows which, in the course of her religious progress, she had experienced; but she was fully sensible that there is far more in real religion than mere occasional transition from one frame of mind and spirit to another. She believed that the experimental acquaintance of the heart with God principally consisted in so living upon Christ by faith, as to aim at living like Him by love. She knew that the love of God towards the sinner and the path of duty prescribed to the sinner, are both of an unchangeable nature. In a believing dependence on the one, and an affectionate walk in the other, she sought and found 'the peace of God which passeth all understanding'; 'for so He giveth His beloved rest.'

She had read but few books besides her Bible; but these few were excellent in their kind, and she spoke of their contents as one who knew their value. In addition *to a Bible and Prayerbook,* Doddridge's *Rise and Progress,* Romaine's *Life, Walk, and Triumph of Faith,* Bunyan's *Pilgrim,* Alleine's *Alarm,* Baxter's *Saints' Everlasting Rest,* a hymn-book, and a few tracts, completed her library.

I observed in her countenance a pale and delicate hue, which I afterwards found to be a presage of consumption; and the idea then occurred to me that she would not live very long.

Time passed on swiftly with this interesting family; and after having partaken of some plain and wholesome refreshment, and enjoyed a few hours' conversation with them, I found it was necessary for me to return homewards. The disposition and character of the parties may be in some sort ascertained by the expressions at parting.

'God send you safe home again,' said the aged mother, 'and bless the day that brought you to see two poor old creatures, such as we are, in our trouble and affliction. Come again, Sir, come again when you can; and though I am a poor ignorant soul, and not fit to talk to such a gentleman as you, yet my dear child shall speak for me;

she is the greatest comfort I have left, and I hope the good Lord will spare her to support my trembling limbs and feeble spirits, till I lie down, with my other dear departed children in the grave.'

'Trust to the Lord,' I answered, 'and remember His gracious promise: "Even to your old age I am He; and even to hoar hairs I will carry you."'

'I thank you, Sir,' said the daughter, 'for your Christian kindness to me and my friends. I believe the blessing of the Lord has attended your visit, and I hope I have experienced it to be so. My dear father and mother will, I am sure, remember it; and I rejoice in the opportunity of seeing so kind a friend under this roof. My Saviour has been abundantly good to me in plucking me as "a brand from the burning," and showing me the way of life and peace; and I hope it is my heart's desire to live to His glory. But I long to see these dear friends enjoy the power and comfort of religion likewise.'

'I think it evident,' I replied, 'that the promise is fulfilled in their case: "It shall come to pass, that at evening time it shall be light."'

'I believe it,' she said, 'and praise God for the blessed hope.'

'Thank Him, too, that you have been the happy instrument of bringing them to the light.'

'I do, Sir; yet when I think of my own unworthiness and insufficiency, I rejoice with trembling.'

'Sir,' said the good old man, 'I am sure the Lord will reward you for this kindness. Pray for us, old as we are, and sinners as we have been, that yet He would have mercy upon us at the eleventh hour. Poor Betsy strives much for our sakes, both in body and soul: she works hard all day to save us trouble, and I fear has not strength to support all she does; and then she talks to us, and reads to us, and prays for us, that we may be saved from the wrath to come. Indeed, Sir, she's a rare child to us.'

'Peace be to you and to all that belong to you!'

'Amen, and thank you, dear Sir,' was echoed from each tongue.

Thus we parted for that time. My returning meditations were sweet, and, I hope, profitable.

Many other visits were afterwards made by me to this peaceful cottage, and I always found increasing reason to thank God for the intercourse I there enjoyed. An interval of some length occurred once during that year, in which I had not seen the Dairyman's family. I was reminded of the circumstance by the receipt of the following letter: —

'REV. SIR,

'I have been expecting to see or hear from you for a considerable time. Excuse the liberty I take in sending you another letter. I have been confined to the house the greater part of the time since I left ——. I took cold that day, and have been worse ever since. I walk out a little on these fine days, but seem to myself to walk very near the borders of eternity. Glory be to God, it is a very pleasing prospect before me! Though I feel the working of sin, and am abased, yet Jesus shows His mercy to be mine, and I trust that I am His. At such times,

"My soul would leave this heavy clay
    At His transporting word,
Run up with joy the shining way
    To meet and prove the Lord.

"Fearless of hell and ghastly death,
    I'd break through every foe;
The wings of love and arms of faith

30

Should bear me captive through."

'My desire is to live every moment to God, that I may, through His grace, be kept in that heavenly, happy frame of mind that I shall wish for at the hour of death. We cannot live or die happy without this; and to keep it, we must be continually watching and praying: for we have many enemies to disturb our peace. I am so very weak that now I can go nowhere to any outward means for that help which is so refreshing to my spirit.

'I should have been very happy to have heard you last Sunday, when you preached at——: I could not walk so far. I hope the word spoken by you was made a blessing to many who heard it. It was my earnest prayer to God that it might be so. But, alas! once calling does not awaken many that are in a sound sleep, yet the voice of God is sometimes very powerful, when His ministers speak; when they arc influenced by His Holy Spirit, and are simple and sincere in holding forth the word of life. Then it will teach us all things, and enlighten our mind and reveal unto us the hidden things of darkness, and give us out of that divine treasure "things new and old." Resting on God to work in us both to will and to do of His own good pleasure, we ought always to work as diligent servants, that know they have a good Master, Who will surely not forget their labour of love.

'If we could but fix our eyes always on that crown of glory that waits us in the skies, we should never grow weary in well-doing; but should run with patience and delight in the work and ways of God, where He appoints us. We should not then, as we too frequently do, suffer these trifling objects here on earth to draw away our minds from God, to rob Him of His glory, and our souls of that happiness and comfort which the believer may enjoy amidst outward afflictions. If we thus lived more by faith

31

in the Son of God, we should endeavour to stir up all whom we could to seek after God. We should tell them what He has done for us, and what He would do for them, if they truly sought Him. We should show them what a glorious expectation there is for all true believers and sincere seekers.

'When our minds are so fixed on God, we are more desirous of glorifying Him, in making known His goodness to us, than the proud rich man is of getting honour to himself. I mourn over my own backwardness to this exercise of duty, when I think of God's willingness to save the vilest of the vile, according to the dispensations of His eternal grace and mercy. Oh, how amiable, how lovely, does this make that God of love appear to poor sinners, that can view Him as such! How is the soul delighted with such a contemplation! They that have much forgiven, how much they love!

'These thoughts have been much on my mind since the death of ——. I trust the Lord will pardon me for neglect. I thought it was my duty to speak or write to him; you remember what I said to you respecting it. But I still delayed till a more convenient season. Oh, how I was struck when I heard the Lord had taken him so suddenly! I was filled with sorrow and shame for having neglected what I had so often resolved to do. But now the time of speaking for God to him was over. Hence we see that the Lord's time is the best time. Now the night of death was come upon him; no more work was to be done. If I had done all that lay in my power to proclaim reconciliation by Christ to his soul, whether he had heard or no, I should have been clear of his blood, but I cannot recall the time that is past, nor him from the grave. Had I known the Lord would have called him so suddenly, how diligent I should have been to warn him of his danger! But it is enough that God shows us what we are to do, and not what He is about to do with us or any of His creatures. Pray, Sir, do all you can for the glory of God. The time will soon pass by, and then we shall enter that glorious rest that He hath prepared for them that love Him. I pray God to fill you with that zeal and love which He only can inspire, that you may daily win souls to Christ. May He deliver you from all slavish fear of man, and give you boldness, as He did of old those that were filled with the Holy Ghost and with power!

'Remember, Christ hath promised to be with all His faithful ministers to the end of time. The greater dangers and difficulties they are exposed to, the more powerful His assistance. Then, Sir, let us fear none but Him. I hope you will pray much for me, a poor sinner, that God will perfect His strength in my weakness of body and mind; for without Him I can do nothing. But when I can experience the teaching of that Holy One, I need no other teacher. May the Lord anoint you with the same, and give you every grace of His Holy Spirit, that you may be filled with all the fulness of God: that you may know what is the height and depth, the length and breadth, of the love of God in Christ Jesus: that you may be in the hand of the Lord, as a keen archer to draw the bow, while the Lord directs and fastens the arrows of conviction in the hearts of such as are under your ministry!

'I sincerely pray that you may be made a blessing to him that has taken the place of the deceased. I have heard that you are fellow-countrymen: I hope you are, however, both as strangers in this world, that have no abiding place, but seek a country out of sight.

'Pray excuse all faults, from

'your humble servant in the

'bonds of the gospel of Christ.

'E——W——.'

33

When I perused this and other letters, which were at different times written to me by the Dairyman's daughter, I felt that in the person of this interesting correspondent were singularly united the characters of a humble disciple and a faithful monitor. I wished to acknowledge the goodness of God in each of these her capacities.

I sometimes entertain a hope that the last day will unfold the value of these epistolary communications beyond even any present estimate of their spiritual importance.

PART IV.

THE DAIRYMAN BEARS AN URGENT MESSAGE

THE TRANSLATION of sinners 'from the power of darkness into the kingdom of God's dear Son,' is the joy of Christians and the admiration of angels. Every penitent and pardoned soul is a new witness to the triumphs of the Redeemer over sin, death, and the grave. How great the change that is wrought! The child of wrath becomes a monument of grace—a brand plucked from the burning! 'If any man be in Christ, he is a new creature: old things are passed away: behold all things are become new.' How marvellous, how interesting, is the spiritual history of each individual believer! He is, like David, 'a wonder to many,' but the greatest wonder of all to himself. Others may doubt whether it be so or not; but to him it is unequivocally proved, that, from first to last, grace alone reigns in the work of his salvation.

The character and privileges of real Christians are beautifully described in the language of our Church; which, when speaking of the objects of divine favour and compassion, says: 'They that be endued with so excellent a benefit of God, be called, according to God's purpose in due season: they through grace obey the calling: they be justified freely: they be made sons of God by adoption: they be made like the image of His only begotten Son, Jesus Christ: they walk religiously in good works; and at length, by God's mercy, they attain to everlasting felicity.'

Such a conception and display of the Almighty wisdom, power, and love, is indeed 'full of sweet, pleasant, and unspeakable comfort to godly persons, and such as feel in themselves the working of the Spirit of Christ mortifying the works of the flesh, and their earthly members, and drawing up their minds to high and heavenly things: it doth greatly establish and confirm their faith of eternal salvation, to be enjoyed through Christ, and doth fervently kindle their love towards God.'

Nearly allied to the consolation of a good hope through grace, as it respects our own personal state before God, is that of seeing its evidences shed lustre over the disposition and conduct of others. Bright was the exhibition of the union between true Christian enjoyment and Christian exertion, in the character whose moral and spiritual features I am attempting to delineate.

It seemed to be the first wish of her heart to prove to others what God had already proved to her, that Jesus is, 'the way, the truth, and the life.' She desired to evince the reality of her calling, justification, and adoption into the family of God, by showing a conformity to the image of Christ, and by walking 'religiously in good works': she trusted that, in this path of faith and obedience, she should 'at length, by God's mercy, attain to everlasting felicity.'

I had the spiritual charge of another parish, adjoining to that in which I resided. It was a small district, and had but few inhabitants. The church was pleasantly situated on a rising bank, at the foot of a considerable hill. It was surrounded by trees, and had a rural, retired appearance. Close to the churchyard stood a large old mansion, which had formerly been the residence of an opulent and titled family; but it had long since been appropriated to the use of the estate as a farm-house. Its outward aspect bore considerable remains of ancient grandeur, and gave a pleasing character to the spot of ground on which the church stood.

In every direction the roads that led to this house of God possessed distinct but interesting features. One of them ascended between several rural cottages, from the sea-shore, which adjoined the lower part of the village street. Another winded round the curved sides of the adjacent hill, and was adorned, both above and below, with numerous sheep, feeding on the herbage of the down. A third road led to the church by a gently rising approach, between high banks, covered with young trees, bushes, ivy, hedge-plants, and wild flowers.

From a point of land which commanded a view of all these several avenues, I used sometimes for a while to watch my congregation gradually assembling together at the hour of Sabbath worship. They were in some directions visible for a considerable distance. Gratifying associations of thought would form in my mind, as I contemplated their approach, and successive arrival, within the precincts of the house of prayer.

One day as I was thus occupied, during a short interval previous to the hour of divine service, I reflected on the joy which David experienced, at the time he exclaimed: 'I was glad when they said unto me, Let us go into the house of the Lord. Our feet shall stand within thy gates, O Jerusalem. Jerusalem is builded as a city that is compact together; whither the tribes go up, the tribes of the Lord, unto the testimony of Israel, to give thanks unto the name of the Lord.'

I was led to reflect upon the various blessings connected with the establishment of public worship. How many immortal souls are now gathering together to perform the all-important work of prayer and praise—to hear the word of God—to feed upon the bread of life! They are leaving their respective dwellings, and will soon be united together in the house of prayer. How beautifully does this represent the effect produced by the voice of the 'Good Shepherd,' calling His sheep from every part of the wilderness into His fold! As these fields, hills, and lanes, are now covered with men, women, and children, in various directions, drawing nearer to each other, and to the object of their journey's end; even so many 'shall come from the east, and from the west, and from the north, and from the south, and shall sit down in the kingdom of God.'

Who can rightly appreciate the value of such hours as these?—hours spent in learning the ways of holy pleasantness and the paths of heavenly peace—hours devoted to the service of God and of souls; in warning the sinner to flee from the wrath to come; in teaching the ignorant how to live and die; in preaching the gospel to the poor; in healing the brokenhearted; in declaring 'deliverance to the captives, and recovering of sight to the blind.'—'Blessed is the people that know the joyful sound: they shall walk, O Lord, in the light of Thy countenance. In Thy name they shall rejoice all the day, and in Thy righteousness shall they be exalted.'

My thoughts then pursued a train of reflection on the importance of the ministerial office, as connected in the purposes of God with the salvation of sinners. I inwardly prayed that those many individuals whom He had given me to instruct, might not, through my neglect or error, be as sheep having no shepherd, nor as the blind led by the blind; but rather that I might, in season and out of season, faithfully proclaim the simple and undisguised truths of the gospel to the glory of God and the prosperity of His Church.

At that instant, near the bottom of the enclosed lane which led to the churchyard, I observed a friend, whom, at such a distance from his home, I little expected to meet. It was the venerable Dairyman. He came up the ascent, leaning with one hand on his trusty staff, and with the other on the arm of a younger man, well known to me, who appeared to be much gratified in meeting with such a companion by the way.

My station was on the top of one of the banks which formed the hollow road beneath. They passed a few yards below me. I was concealed from their sight by a projecting tree. They were talking of the mercies of God, and the unsearchable riches of His grace. The Dairyman was telling his companion what a blessing the Lord had given him in his daughter. His countenance brightened as he named her, and called her his precious Betsy.

I met them at a stile not many yards beyond, and accompanied them to the church, which was hard by.

'Sir,' said the old man. 'I have brought a letter from my daughter. I hope I am in time for divine service. Seven miles has now become a long walk for me: I grow old and weak. I am very glad to see you, Sir.'

'How is your daughter?'

'Very poorly indeed, Sir—very poorly. The doctors say it is a decline. I sometimes hope she will get the better of it; but then, again I have many fears. You know, Sir, that I have cause to love and prize her. Oh! it would be such a trial: but the Lord knows what is best. Excuse my weakness, Sir.'

He put a letter into my hand, the perusal of which I reserved till afterwards, as the time was nigh for going into church.

The presence of this aged pilgrim, the peculiar reverence and affection with which he joined in the different parts of the service, excited many gratifying thoughts in my mind; such as rather furthered than interrupted devotion.

The train of reflection in which I had been engaged, when I first discovered him on the road, at intervals recurred powerfully to my feelings, as I viewed that very congregation assembled together in the house of God, whose steps, in their approach towards it, I had watched with prayerful emotions.

'Here the rich and poor met together in mutual acknowledgement, that the Lord is the Maker of them all; and that all are alike dependent creatures, looking up to one common Father to supply their wants, both temporal and spiritual.

'Again, likewise will they meet together in the grave, that undistinguished receptacle of the opulent and the needy.

'And once more, at the judgment seat of Christ, shall the rich and the poor meet together, that "everyone may receive the things done in his body, according to that he hath done, whether it be good or bad."

'How closely connected in the history of man are these three periods of a general meeting together!

'The house of prayer—the house appointed for all living—and the house not made with hands, eternal in the heavens. May we never separate these ideas from each other, but retain them in a sacred and profitable union! So shall our worshipping assemblies on earth be representative of the general assembly and church of the first-born, which are written in heaven.'

When the congregation dispersed, I entered into discourse with the Dairyman and a few of the poor of my flock, whose minds were of the like disposition to his own. He seldom could speak long together without some reference to his dear child. He loved to tell how merciful his God had been to him, in the dutiful and affectionate attentions of his daughter. All real Christians feel a tender spiritual attachment towards those who have been the instrument of bringing them to an effectual knowledge of the way of salvation: but when that instrument is one so nearly allied, how dear does the relationship become!

If my friend the Dairyman was in any danger of falling into idolatry, his child would have been the idol of his affections. She was the prop and stay of her parents' declining years, and they scarcely knew how sufficiently to testify the gratitude of their hearts, for the comfort and blessing which she was the means of affording them.

While he was relating several particulars of his family history to the others, I opened and read the following letter:

'SIR,

'Once more I take the liberty to trouble you with a few lines. I received your letter with great pleasure, and thank you for it. I am now so weak, that I am unable to walk to any public place of divine worship, a privilege which has heretofore always so much strengthened and refreshed me. I used to go in anxious expectation to meet my God, and hold sweet communion with Him, and I was seldom disappointed. In the means of grace, all the channels of divine mercy are open to every heart that is lifted up to receive out of that divine fulness grace for grace. These are the times of refreshing from the presence of the Lord. How have I rejoiced to hear a faithful and lively messenger, just come, as it were, from communion with God at the throne of grace, with his heart warmed and filled with divine love, to speak to fallen sinners! Such a one has seemed to me as if his face shone as that of Moses did with the glory of God, when he came down from the mount, where he had been within the veil. May you, Sir, imitate him, as he did Christ, that all may see and know that the Lord dwelleth with you, and that you dwell in Him through the unity of the blessed Spirit. I trust you are no stranger to His divine teaching, aid, and assistance, in all you set your hand to do for the glory of God.

'I hope, Sir, the sincerity of my wishes for your spiritual welfare will plead an excuse for the freedom of my address to you. I pray the Giver of every perfect gift, that you may experience the mighty workings of His

gracious Spirit in your heart and your ministry, and rest
your all on the justifying and purifying blood of an expired
Redeemer. Then will you triumph in His strength, and be
enabled to say with the poet—

> "Shall I, through fear of feeble man,
> The Spirit's course strive to restrain?
> Or, undismay'd in deed and word,
> Be a true witness for my Lord?
>
> "Aw'd by a mortal's frown, shall I
> Conceal the word of God most high?
> How then before Thee shall I dare
> To stand, or how Thine anger bear?
>
> "Shall I, to soothe th' unholy throng,
> Soften Thy truths and smooth Thy tongue
> To gain earth's gilded toys, or flee
> The cross endur'd, my God, by Thee?
>
> "What then is he, whose scorn I dread?
> Whose wrath or hate makes me afraid?
> A man? an heir of death? a slave
> To sin? a bubble on the wave?
>
> "Yea, let men rage, since Thou wilt spread
> Thy shadowing wings around my head;
> Since in all pain Thy tender love
> Will still my sure refreshment prove.
>
> "Still shall the love of Christ constrain
> To seek the wand'ring souls of men,
> With cries, entreaties, tears to save,
> And snatch them from the yawning grave.

"For this let men revile thy name,
No cross I shun, I fear no shame:
All hall reproach, and welcome pain,
Only Thy terrors, Lord, restrain."

'I trust, Sir, that you see what a glorious high calling yours is, and that you are one of those who walk humbly with God, that you may be taught of Him in all things. Persons in your place are messengers of the most high God. Is it too much to say, they should live like the angels in all holiness, and be filled with love and zeal for men's souls? They are ambassadors, in Christ's stead, to persuade sinners to be reconciled to God. So that your calling is above that of angels: for they are *afterwards* to minister to the heirs of salvation; but the sinner must be *first* reconciled to God. And you are called on from day to day to intercede with man as his friend, that you may win souls to Christ. Christ is ascended up on high, to intercede with His Father for guilty sinners, and to plead for them the merits of His death. So that Christ and His faithful ministers, through the operation of the blessed Spirit, are co-workers together. Yet without Him we can do nothing; our strength is His strength, and His is all the glory from first to last.

'It is my heart's prayer and desire, Sir, that you may, by a living faith, cleave close to that blessed exalted Lamb of God, who died to redeem us from sin—that you may have a sweet communion with Father, Son, and Spirit—that you may sink deep in humble love, and rise high in the life of God. Thus will you have such discoveries of the beauties of Christ and His eternal glory, as will fill your heart with true delight.

'If I am not deceived, I wish myself to enjoy His gracious favour, more than all the treasures which earth can afford. I would in comparison look upon them with holy disdain, and as not worth an anxious thought, that they may not have power on my heart to draw or attract it from God, who is worthy of my highest esteem, and of all my affections. It should be our endeavour to set Him alway before us, that in all things we may act as in His immediate presence: that we may be filled with that holy fear, so that we may not dare wilfully to sin against Him. We should earnestly entreat the Lord to mortify the power and working of sin and unbelief within us, by making Christ appear more and more precious in our eyes, and more dear to our hearts.

'It fills my heart with thankful recollections, while I attempt in this weak manner to speak of God's love to man. When I reflect on my past sins, and His past mercies, I am assured, that if I had all the gifts of wise men and angels, I could never sufficiently describe my own inward sense of His undeserved love towards me. We can better enjoy these glorious apprehensions in our hearts, than explain them to others. But, oh, how unworthy of them all we are! Consciousness of my own corruption keeps me often low; yet faith and desire will easily mount on high, beseeching God that He would, according to the apostle's prayer, fill me with all His communicable fulness, in the gifts and graces of His Spirit; that I may walk well-pleasing before Him, in all holy conversation, perfecting holiness in His fear.

'If I err in boldness, Sir, pray pardon me, and in your next letter confirm my hope that you will be my counsellor and guide.

'I can only recompense your kindness to me by my prayers, that your own intercourse with God may be abundantly blessed to you and yours. I consider the Saviour saying to you, as He did to Peter, "Lovest thou Me?" And may your heartfelt experience be compelled to reply, "Thou knowest all things, and Thou knowest that I love Thee" supremely! May He have evident marks of it in all your outward actions of love and humanity, in feeding His flock, and in the inward fervour and affection of all your consecrated powers: that you may be zealously engaged in pulling down the strongholds of sin and Satan, and building up His Church; sowing the seeds of righteousness, and praying God to give the increase: that you may not labour for Him in vain; but may see the trees bud and blossom, and bring forth fruit abundantly, to the praise and glory of your heavenly Master. In order to give you encouragement, He says, whosoever "converteth a sinner from the error of his way, shall save a soul from death"; and that will increase the brightness of your crown in glory. This hath Christ merited for His faithful ministers.

'I hope, Sir, you will receive grace to be sincere in reproving sin, wherever you see it. You will find divine assistance, and all fear and shame taken from you. Great peace will be given to you, and wisdom, strength, and courage, according to your work. You will be as Paul; having much learning, you can speak to men in all stations in life, by God's assistance. The fear of offending them will never prevent you, when you consider the glory of God; and man's immortal soul is of more value than his present favour and esteem. In particular, you are in an office wherein you can visit all the sick. Man's extremity is often God's opportunity. In this way you may prove an instrument in His hand to do His work. Although He can work without means, yet His usual way is by means; and I trust you are a chosen vessel unto Him, to prove His name and declare His truth to all men.

'Visiting the sick is a strict command, and a duty for every Christian. None can tell what good may be done. I wish it was never neglected, as it too often is. Many think, that if they attend in the church, the minister to preach, and the people to hear, their duty is done. But more is required than this. May the Lord stir up the gift that is in His people and ministers, that they may have compassion on their fellow-sinners, that they may never think it too late, but remember that, while there is life, there is hope!

'Once more, I pray, Sir, pardon and excuse all my errors in judgment, and the ignorance that this is penned in; and may God bless you in all things, and particularly your friendship to me and my parents! What a comfort is family religion! I do not doubt but this is your desire, as it is mine, to say,

> "I and my house will serve the Lord,
> But first obedient to His word
>   I must myself appear;
> By actions, words, and tempers show
> That I my heavenly Master know,
>   And serve with heart sincere.

> "I must the fair example set,
> From those that on my pleasure wait
>   The stumbling-block remove;
> Their duty by my life explain,
> And still in all my works maintain
>   The dignity of love.

> "Easy to be entreated, mild,
> Quickly appeased and reconciled,
>   A follower of my God:
> A saint, indeed, I long to be,
> And lead my faithful family
>   In the celestial road.

"Lord, if Thou dost the wish infuse,
A vessel fitted for Thy use
    Into Thy hands receive:
Work in me both to will and do,
And show them how believers true
    And real Christians live.

"With all-sufficient grace supply,
And then I'll come to testify
    The wonders of Thy name,
Which saves from sin, the world and hell:
Its power may every sinner tell,
    And every tongue proclaim!

"Cleansed by the blood of Christ from sin,
I seek my relatives to win,
    And preach their sins forgiven;
Children, and wife, and servants seize,
And through the paths of pleasantness
    Conduct them all to heaven."

'Living so much in a solitary way, books are my companions; and poetry which speaks of the love of God and the mercies of Christ, is very sweet to my mind. This must be my excuse for troubling you to read verses which others have written. I have intended, if my declining state of health permit, to go to —— for a few days. I say this, lest you should call in expectation of seeing me, during any part of next week. But my dear father and mother, for whose precious souls I am very anxious, will reap the benefit of your visit at all events. From
        'Your humble and unworthy servant,
            'E—W—.'

47

Having read it, I said to the father of my highly valued correspondent:

'I thank you for being the bearer of this letter. Your daughter is a kind friend and faithful counsellor to me, as well as to you. Tell her how highly I esteem her friendship, and that I feel truly obliged for the many excellent sentiments which she has here expressed. Give her my blessing, and assure her that the oftener she writes, the more thankful I shall be.'

The Dairyman's enlivened eye gleamed with pleasure as I spoke. The praise of his Elizabeth was a string which could not be touched without causing every nerve of his whole frame to vibrate.

His voice half faltered, as he spoke in reply; the tear started in his eyes; his hand trembled as I pressed it; his heart was full; he could only say:

'Sir, a poor old man thanks you for your kindness to him and his family. God bless you, Sir; I hope we shall soon see you again.'

Thus we parted for that day.

PART V.

PORTRAITS OF A BEAUTIFUL MIND

IT HAS not unfrequently been observed, that when it is the Lord's pleasure to remove any of his faithful followers out of this life at an early period of their course, they make rapid progress in the experience of divine truth. The fruits of the Spirit ripen fast, as they advance to the close of mortal existence. In particular, they grow in humility, through a deeper sense of inward corruption, and a clearer view of the perfect character of the Saviour. Disease and bodily weakness make the thoughts of eternity recur with frequency and power. The great question of their own personal salvation, the quality of their faith, the sincerity of their love, and the purity of their hope, are in continual exercise.

Unseen realities, at such a time, occupy a larger portion of thought than before. The state of existence beyond the grave, the invisible world, the unaltered character of the dead, the future judgment, the total separation from everything earthly, the dissolution of body and spirit, and their re-union at the solemn hour of resurrection—these are subjects for their meditation, which call for serious earnestness of soul. Whatever consolations from the Spirit of God they may have enjoyed heretofore, they become now doubly anxious to examine and prove themselves, whether they be indeed in the faith. In doing this, they sometimes pass through hidden conflicts of a dark and distressing nature from which, however, they come forth like gold tried in the furnace. Awhile they may sow in tears, but soon they reap in joy.

Their religious feelings have then, perhaps, less of ecstacy, but more of serenity.

As the ears of corn ripen for the harvest, they bow their heads nearer to the ground. So it is with believers: they then see more than ever of their own imperfection, and often express their sense of it in strong language; yet they repose with a growing confidence on the love of God through Christ Jesus. The nearer they advance to their eternal rest, the more humble they become, but not the less useful in their sphere. They feel anxiously desirous of improving every talent they possess, to the glory of God, knowing that the time is short.

I thought I observed the truth of these remarks fulfilled in the progressive state of mind of the Dairyman's daughter.

Declining health seemed to indicate the will of God concerning her. But her character, conduct, and experience of the divine favour, increased in brightness as the setting sun of her mortal life approached its horizon. The last letter which, with the exception of a very short note, I ever received from her, I shall now transcribe. It appeared to me to bear the marks of still deeper acquaintance with the workings of her own heart, and a more entire reliance upon the free mercy of God.

The original, while I copy it, strongly revives the image of the deceased, and the many profitable conversations which I once enjoyed in her company and that of her parents. It again endears to me the recollections of cottage piety, and helps me to anticipate the joys of that day when the spirits of the glorified saints shall be reunited to their bodies, and be for ever with the Lord.

The writer of this and the preceding letters herself little imagined, when they were penned, that they would ever be submitted to the public eye; that they now are so from a conviction that the friends of the pious poor will estimate them according to their value, and hope that it may please God to honour these memorials of the dead, to the effectual edification of the living.

'REV. SIR.

'In consequence of your kind permission. I take the liberty to trouble you with another of my ill-written letters; and I trust you have too much of your blessed Master's lowly, meek, and humble mind, to be offended with a poor, simple, ignorant creature whose intentions are pure and sincere in writing. My desire is, that I, a weak vessel of His grace, may glorify His name for His goodness towards me. May the Lord direct me by His counsel and wisdom! May He overshadow me with His presence; that I may sit beneath the banner of His love, and find the consolations of His blessed Spirit sweet and refreshing to my soul!

'When I feel that I am nothing, and God is All in all, then I can willingly fly to Him, saying, "Lord, help me; Lord, teach me; be unto me my Prophet, Priest, and King. Let me know the teaching of Thy grace, and the disclosing of Thy love."

What nearness of access might we have, if we lived more near to God! What sweet communion might we have with a God of love! He is the Great I AM. How glorious a name! Angels with trembling awe prostrate themselves before Him, and in humble love adore and worship Him. One says,

"While the first archangel sings,
He hides his face behind his wings."

Unworthy as I am, I have found it by experience, that the more I see of the greatness and goodness of God, and the nearer union I hope I have had with him through the Spirit of His love, the more humble and self-abased I have been.

'But every day I may say, "Lord, how little I love Thee, how far I live from Thee, how little am I like Thee in humility!" It is nevertheless my heart's desire to love and serve Him better. I find the way in which God does more particularly bless me is when I attend on the public ordinances of religion. These are the channels through which He conveys the riches of His grace and precious love to my soul. These I have often found to be indeed the time of refreshing and strengthening from the presence of the Lord. Then I can see my hope of an interest in the covenant of His love, and praise Him for His mercy to the greatest of sinners.

'I earnestly wish to be more established in His ways, and to honour Him in the path of duty, whilst I enjoy the smiles of His favour. In the midst of all outward afflictions I pray that I may know Christ, and the power of His resurrection within my soul. If I were always thus, my summer would last all the year; my will would then be sweetly lost in God's will, and I should feel a resignation in every dispensation of His providence and His grace, saying, "Good is the will of the Lord: Infinite Wisdom cannot err." Then would patience have its perfect work.

'But, alas! sin and unbelief often, too often, interrupt these frames, and lay me low before God in tears of sorrow. I often think what a happiness it would be, if His love were so fixed in my heart, that I might willingly obey Him with alacrity and delight, and gradually mortify the power of self-will, passion, and pride. This can only arise from a good hope through grace, that we are washed in that precious blood which cleanses us from every sinful stain, and makes us new creatures in Christ. Oh that we may be the happy witnesses of the saving power and virtue of that healing stream which flows from the fountain of everlasting love!

'Sir, my faith is often exceedingly weak: can you be so kind as to tell me what you have found to be the most effectual means of strengthening it? I often think how plainly the Lord declares. Believe only, and thou shalt be saved. Only have faith; all things are possible to him that has it. How I wish that we could remove all those mountains that hinder and obstruct the light of His grace; so that having full access unto God through that ever-blessed Spirit, we might lovingly commune with Him as with the dearest of friends. What favour does God bestow on worms! And yet we love to murmur and complain. He may well say, What should I have done more, that I, have not done? or wherein have I proved unfaithful or unkind to My faithless, backsliding children?

'Sir, I pray that I may not grieve Him, as I have done, any more. I want your counsel and your prayers for me in this matter. How refreshing is the sight of one that truly loves God, that bears His image and likeness!

'But delightful as is conversation with true believers on earth, whose hearts are lifted up to things above, yet what is this to that happy day which will admit us into more bright realms; where we shall for ever behold a God of Jove in the smiling face of His Son, who is the express image of His Father, and the brightness of His glory! Then, if we be found in Him, we shall be received by the innumerable host of angels who wait round His throne. 'In the meantime, Sir, may I take up my cross, and manfully fight under Him who, for the glory that was set before Him, endured the cross, despising the shame, and is now set down at His Father's right hand in majesty! I thank you for the kind liberty you have given me of writing to you. I feel my health declining, and I find a relief, during an hour of pain and weakness, in communicating these thoughts to you.

'I hope, Sir, you go on your way rejoicing; that you are enabled to thank Him who is the Giver of every good gift, spiritual, temporal, and providential, for blessings to yourself and your ministry. I do not doubt but you often meet with circumstances which are not pleasing to nature. Yet, by the blessing of God, they will be all profitable in the end. They are kindly designed by grace to make and keep us humble. The difficulties which you spoke of to me some time since will, I trust, disappear.

'My dear father and mother are as well as usual in bodily health, and I hope grow in grace, and in the knowledge and love of Jesus Christ. My chief desire to live is for their sakes. It now seems long since we have seen you. I am almost ashamed to request you to come to our little cottage to visit those who are so much below your station in life. But if you cannot come, we shall be very glad if you will write a few lines. I ought to make an excuse for my letter. I spell so badly: this was a great neglect when I was young. I gave myself greatly to reading, but not to the other, and now I am too weak and feeble to learn much.

'I hear sometimes of persons growing serious in your congregation. It gives me joy, and if true, I am sure it does so to yourself. I long for the pure gospel of Christ to be preached in every church in the world, and for the time when all shall know, love, and fear the Lord; and the uniting Spirit of God shall make them of one heart and mind in Christ our great Head. Your greatest joy, I know, will be in labouring much for the glory of God in the salvation of men's souls. You serve a good Master. You have a sure reward. I pray God to give you strength according to your day.

'Pray, Sir, do not be offended at the freedom and manner of my writing. My parents' duty and love to you are sent with these lines from
'Your humble servant in Christ,
'E——W——.'

Epistolary communications, when written in sincerity of heart, afford genuine portraits of the mind. May the foregoing be viewed with Christian candour, and consecrated to affectionate memory!

PART VI.

THE ORNAMENTS OF A MEEK SPIRIT

TRAVELLERS, as they pass through the country, usually stop to inquire whose are the splendid mansions which they discover among the woods and plains around them. The families, titles, fortune, or character of the respective owners, engage much attention. Perhaps their houses are exhibited to the admiring stranger. The elegant rooms, costly furniture, valuable paintings, beautiful gardens and shrubberies, are universally approved; while the rank, fashion, taste, and riches of the possessor, afford ample materials for entertaining discussion. In the meantime, the lowly cottage of the poor husbandman is passed by as scarcely deserving of notice. Yet perchance such a cottage may often contain a treasure of infinitely more value than the sumptuous palace of the rich man; even 'the pearl of great price.' If this be set in the heart of the poor cottager, it proves a gem of unspeakable worth, and will shine amongst the brightest ornaments of the Redeemer's crown, in that day when He maketh up His 'jewels.'

Hence, the Christian traveller, while in common with others he bestows his due share of applause on the decorations of the rich, and is not insensible to the beauties and magnificence which are the lawfully allowed appendages of rank and fortune, cannot overlook the humbler dwelling of the poor. And if he should find that true piety and grace beneath the thatched roof which he has in vain looked for amidst the worldly grandeur of the rich, he remembers the declarations in the Word of God.

He sees with admiration, that the high and lofty One that inhabiteth eternity, Whose name is Holy, Who dwelleth in the high and holy place, dwelleth with him also that is of a contrite and humble spirit (Isa. lvii. 15); and although heaven is His throne, and the earth His footstool, yet, when a house is to be built, and a place of rest to be sought for Himself, He says, 'To this man will I look, even to him that is poor and of a contrite spirit, and trembleth at My word' (Isa. lxvi. 2.).

When a house is thus tenanted, faith beholds this inscription written on the walls, *The Lord lives here*. Faith therefore cannot pass it by unnoticed, but loves to lift up the latch of the door, and to sit down and converse with the poor, although perhaps despised, inhabitant. Many a sweet interview does faith obtain, when she thus takes her walks abroad. Many such a sweet interview have I myself enjoyed beneath the roof where dwelt the Dairyman and his little family.

I soon perceived that his daughter's health was rapidly on the decline. The pale, wasting consumption, which is the Lord's instrument for removing so many thousands every year from the land of the living, made hasty strides on her constitution. The hollow eye, the distressing cough, and the often too fluttering flush on the cheek, foretold the approach of death.

What a field for usefulness and affectionate attention, on the part of ministers and Christian friends, is opened by the frequent attacks and lingering process of consumptive illness! How many such precious opportunities are daily lost, where Providence seems in so marked a way to afford time and space for serious and godly instruction! Of how many may it be said, 'The way of peace have they not known!' for not one friend ever came nigh, to warn them to 'flee from the wrath to come.'

But the Dairyman's daughter was happily made acquainted with the things which belonged to her everlasting peace, before the present disease had taken root in her constitution. In my visits to her, I went rather to receive information than to impart it. Her mind was absolutely stored with divine truths, and her conversation was truly edifying. The recollection of it will ever produce a thankful sensation in my heart.

I one day received a short note to the following effect:

'DEAR SIR,

'I should be very glad, if your convenience will allow, that you will come and see a poor unworthy sinner; my hour-glass is nearly run out, but I hope I can see Christ to be precious to my soul. Your conversation has often been blessed to me, and I now feel the need of it more than ever. My father and mother send their duty to you.

From your obedient,

And unworthy servant.

'E——W——.'

I obeyed the summons that same afternoon. On my arrival at the Dairyman's cottage, his wife opened the door. The tears streamed down her cheek, as she silently shook her head. Her heart was full. She tried to speak, but could not. I took her by the hand and said:

'My good friend, all is right, and as the Lord of wisdom and mercy directs.'

'Oh, my Betsy, my dear girl, is so bad, Sir. What shall I do without her?—I thought I should have gone first to the grave; but——'

'But the Lord sees good that before you die yourself you should behold your child safe home to glory. Is there no mercy in this?'

'O dear Sir! I am very old and very weak; and she is a dear child, the staff and prop of a poor old creature, as I am.'

As I advanced, I saw Elizabeth sitting by the fire-side, supported in an arm-chair by pillows, with every mark of rapid decline and approaching death. A sweet smile of friendly complacency enlightened her pale countenance, as she said:

'This is very kind indeed, Sir, to come so soon after I sent to you. You find me daily wasting away, and I cannot have long to continue here. My flesh and my heart fail, but God is the strength of my weak heart, and I trust will be my portion for ever.'

The conversation was occasionally interrupted by her cough and want of breath. Her tone of voice was clear, though feeble: her manner solemn and collected; and her eye, though more dim than formerly, by no means wanting in liveliness as she spoke. I had frequently admired the superior language in which she expressed her ideas, as well as the Scriptural consistency with which she communicated her thoughts. She had a good natural understanding; and grace, as is generally the case, had much improved it. On the present occasion I could not help thinking she was peculiarly favoured. The whole strength of gracious and natural attainments seemed to be in full exercise.

After taking my seat between the daughter and the mother (the latter fixing her fond eyes upon her child with great anxiety while we were conversing), I said to Elizabeth:

'I hope you enjoy a sense of the divine presence, and can rest all upon Him, who has "been with thee, and has kept thee in all places where thou hast gone," and will bring thee into "the land of pure delight, where saints immortal reign."'

'Sir, I think I can. My mind has lately been sometimes clouded, but I believe it has been partly owing to the great weakness and suffering of my bodily frame, and partly to the envy of my spiritual enemy, who wants to persuade me that Christ has no love for me, and that I have been a self-deceiver.'

'And do you give way to his suggestions? Can you doubt, amidst such numerous tokens of past and present mercy?'

'No, Sir, I mostly am enabled to preserve a clear evidence of His love. I do not wish to add to my other sins that of denying His manifest goodness to my soul. I would acknowledge it to His praise and glory.'

'What is your present view of the state in which you were, before you felt seriously concerned about the salvation of your soul?'

'Sir, I was a proud, thoughtless girl, fond of dress and finery; I loved the world, and the things that are in the world. I lived in service among worldly people, and never had the happiness of being in a family where worship was regarded, and the souls of the servants cared for, either by master or mistress. I went once on a Sunday to church, more to see and be seen, than to pray or hear the Word of God. I thought I was quite good enough to be saved; and disliked, and often laughed at, religious people. I was in great darkness; I knew nothing of the way of salvation; I never prayed, nor was sensible of the awful danger of a prayerless state. I wished to maintain the character of a good servant, and was much lifted up whenever I met with applause. I was tolerably moral and decent in my conduct, from motives of carnal and worldly policy; but I was a stranger to God and Christ. I neglected my soul; and had I died in such a state, hell must, and would justly, have been my portion.'

'How long is it since you heard the sermon which you hope, through God's blessing, effected your conversion?'

'About five years ago.'

'How was it brought about?'

'It was reported that a Mr ——, who was detained by contrary winds from embarking on board ship as chaplain to a distant part of the world, was to preach at —— church. Many advised me not to go for fear he should turn my head; as they said he held strange notions. But curiosity, and an opportunity of appearing in a new gown, which I was very proud of, induced me to ask leave of my mistress to go. Indeed, Sir, I had no better motives than vanity and curiosity. Yet thus it pleased the Lord to order it for His own glory.

'I accordingly went to church, and saw a great crowd of people collected together. I often think of the contrary states of my mind during the former and latter part of the service. For a while, regardless of the worship of God, I looked around me, and was anxious to attract notice myself. My dress, like that of too many gay, vain, and silly servant girls, was much above my station, and very different from that which becomes a humble sinner, who has a modest sense of propriety and decency. The state of my mind was visible enough from the foolish finery of my apparel.

'At length the clergyman gave out his text: 'Be ye clothed with humility.' He drew a comparison between the clothing of the body with that of the soul. At a very early part of his discourse I began to feel ashamed of my passion for fine dressing and apparel; but when he came to describe the garment of salvation with which a Christian is clothed. I felt a powerful discovery of the nakedness of my own soul. I saw that I had neither the humility mentioned in the text, nor anyone part of the true Christian character.

I looked at my gay dress, and blushed for shame on account of my pride. I looked at the minister, and he seemed to be as a messenger sent from heaven to open my eyes. I looked at the congregation, and wondered whether anyone else felt as I did. I looked at my heart, and it appeared full of iniquity. I trembled as he spoke, and yet I felt a great drawing of heart to the words he uttered.

'He opened the riches of divine grace in God's method of saving the sinner. I was astonished at what I had been doing all the days of my life. He described the meek, lowly, and humble example of Christ: I felt proud, lofty, vain, and self-consequential. He represented Christ as "Wisdom"; I felt my ignorance. He held Him forth as "Righteousness"; I was convinced of my own guilt. He proved Him to be "Sanctification"; I saw my corruption. He proclaimed Him as "Redemption"; I felt my slavery to sin, and my captivity to Satan. He concluded with an animated address to sinners, in which he exhorted them to flee from the wrath to come, to cast off the love of outward ornaments, to put on Jesus Christ, and be clothed with true humility.

'From that hour I never lost sight of the value of my soul, and the danger of a sinful state. I inwardly blessed God for the sermon, although my mind was in a state of great confusion.

'The preacher had brought forward the ruling passion of my heart, which was pride in outward dress; and by the grace of God it was made instrumental to the awakening of my soul. Happy, Sir, would it be, if many a poor girl, like myself, were turned from the love of outward adorning and putting on of fine apparel, to seek that which is not corruptible, even the ornament of a meek and quiet spirit, which is in the sight of God of great price.

'The greatest part of the congregation, unused to such faithful and Scriptural sermons, disliked and complained of the severity of the preacher: while a few, as I afterwards found, like myself, were deeply affected, and earnestly wished to hear him again. But he preached there no more.

'From that time I was led, through a course of private prayer, reading, and meditation, to see my lost state as a sinner, and the great mercy of God through Jesus Christ, in raising sinful dust and ashes to a share in the glorious happiness of heaven. And, oh, Sir, what a Saviour I have found! He is more than I could ask or desire. In His fulness I have found all that my poverty could need: in His bosom I have found a resting-place from all sin and sorrow; in His word I have found strength against doubt and unbelief.

'Were you not soon convinced,' I said, 'that your salvation must be an act of entire grace on the part of God, wholly independent of your own previous works or deservings?'

'Dear Sir, what were my works, before I heard that sermon, but evil, carnal, selfish, and ungodly? The thoughts of my heart, from my youth upward, were only evil, and that continually. And my deservings, what were they but the deservings of a fallen, depraved, careless soul, that regarded neither law nor gospel? Yes, Sir, I immediately saw that if ever I were saved, it must be by the free mercy of God, and that the whole praise and honour of the work would be His from first to last.' '

'What change did you perceive in yourself with respect to the world?'

'It appeared all vanity and vexation of spirit. I found it necessary to my peace of mind to come out from among them and be separate. I gave myself to prayer; and many a happy hour of secret delight I enjoyed in communion with God. Often I mourned over my sins, and sometimes had a great conflict through unbelief, fear, temptation to return back again to my old ways, and a variety of difficulties which lay in my way. But He who loved me with an everlasting love, drew me by His loving-kindness, showed me the way of peace, gradually strengthened me in my resolutions of leading a new life, and taught me that, while without Him I could do nothing, I yet might do all things through His strength.

'Did you not find many difficulties in your situation, owing to your change of principle and practice?'

'Yes, Sir, every day of my life. I was laughed at by some, scolded at by others, scorned by enemies, and pitied by friends. I was called hypocrite, saint, false deceiver, and many more names which were meant to render me hateful in the sight of the world. But I esteemed the reproach of the cross an honour. I forgave and prayed for my persecutors, and remembered how very lately I had acted the same part towards others myself. I thought also that Christ endured the contradiction of sinners; and, as the disciple is not above his Master, I was glad to be in any way conformed to His sufferings.'

'Did you not then feel for your family at home?'

'Yes, that I did indeed, Sir; they were never out of my thoughts. I prayed continually for them, and had a longing desire to do them good. In particular I felt for my father and mother, as they were getting into years, and were very ignorant and dark in matters of religion.'

'Ay,' interrupted her mother, sobbing, 'ignorant and dark, sinful and miserable we were, till this dear Betsy—this dear Betsy—this dear child, Sir, brought Christ Jesus home to her poor father and mother's house.'

'No, dearest mother, say rather, Christ Jesus brought your poor daughter home to tell you what He had done for her soul, and I hope, to do the same for you.'

At this moment the Dairyman came in with two pails of milk hanging from the yoke on his shoulders. He had stood behind the half-opened door for a few minutes, and heard the last sentences spoken by his wife and daughter.

'Blessing and mercy upon her!' said he, 'it is very true; she left a good place of service on purpose to live with us, that she might help us both in soul and body. Sir, don't she look very ill? I think, Sir, we sha'n't have her here long.'

'Leave that to the Lord,' said Elizabeth. 'All our times are in His hand, and happy it is that they are. I am willing to go; are you not willing, my father, to part with me into His hands who gave me to you at first?'

'Ask me any question in the world but that,' said the weeping father.

'I know,' said she, 'you wish me to be happy.'

'I do, I do,' answered he; 'let the Lord do with you and us as best pleases Him.'

I then asked her on what her present consolations chiefly depended, in the prospect of approaching death.

'Entirely, Sir, on my view of Christ. When I look at myself, many sins, infirmities, and imperfections cloud the image of Christ which I want to see in my own heart. But when I look at the Saviour Himself He is altogether lovely; there is not one spot in His countenance, nor one cloud over all His perfections.

'I think of His coming in the flesh, and it reconciles me to the sufferings of the body; for He had them as well as I. I think of His temptations, and believe that He is able to succour me when I am tempted. Then I think of His cross, and learn to bear my own; I reflect on His death, and long to die unto sin so that it may no longer have dominion over me. I sometimes think on His resurrection, and trust that He has given me a part in it, for I feel that my affections are set upon things above. Chiefly I take comfort in thinking of Him as at the right hand of the

Father, pleading my cause, and rendering acceptable even my feeble prayers, both for myself and, as I hope, for my dear friends.

'These are the views which, through mercy, I have of my Saviour's goodness; and they have made me wish and strive in my poor way to serve Him, to give myself up to Him, and to labour to do my duty in that state of life into which it has pleased God to can me.

'A thousand times I should have fallen and fainted, if He had not upheld me. I feel that I am nothing without Him. He is All in all.

'Just so far as I can cast my care upon Him, I find strength to do His will. May He give me grace to trust Him till the last moment! I do not fear death, because I believe that He has taken away its sting. And oh! what happiness beyond! Tell me, Sir, whether you think I am right. I hope I am under no delusion. I dare not look for my hope in anything short of the entire fulness of Christ. When I ask my own heart a question, I am afraid to trust it, for it is treacherous, and has often deceived me. But when I ask Christ, He answers me with promises that strengthen and refresh me, and leave me no room to doubt His power and will to save. I am in His hands, and would remain there: and I do believe that He will never leave nor forsake me, but will perfect the thing that concerns me. He loved me and gave Himself for me, and I believe that His gifts and callings are without repentance. In this hope I live, in this hope I wish to die.'

I looked around me as she was speaking, and thought, 'Surely this is none other than the house of God, and the gate of heaven.' Everything appeared neat, cleanly, and interesting. The afternoon had been rather overcast with dark clouds; but just now the setting sun shone brightly and somewhat suddenly into the room. It was reflected from three or four rows of bright pewter plates and white earthenware, arranged on shelves against the wall: it also gave brilliancy to a few prints of sacred subjects that hung there also, and served for monitors of the birth, baptism, crucifixion, and resurrection of Christ.

A large map of Jerusalem, and a hieroglyphic of 'the old and new man,' completed the decorations on that side of the room. Clean as was the white-washed wall, it was not cleaner than the rest of the place and its furniture. Seldom had the sun enlightened a house where order and general neatness (those sure attendants of pious poverty) were more conspicuous.

This gleam of setting sunshine was emblematical of the bright and serene close of the young Christian's departing season. One ray happened to be reflected from a little looking-glass upon her face. Amidst her pallid and decaying features there appeared a calm resignation, triumphant confidence, unaffected humility, and tender anxiety, which fully declared the feelings of her heart.

Some further affectionate conversation, and a short prayer, closed this interview.

As I rode home by departing daylight, a solemn tranquility reigned throughout the scene. The gentle lowing of cattle, the bleating of sheep just penned in their folds, the humming of the insects of the night, the distant murmurs of the sea, the last notes of the birds of the day, and the first warblings of the nightingale, broke upon the ear, and served rather to increase than lessen the peaceful serenity of the evening and its corresponding effects on my own mind. It invited and cherished just such meditations as my visit had already inspired. Natural scenery, when viewed in a Christian mirror, frequently affords very beautiful illustrations of divine truths. We are highly favoured when we can enjoy them, and at the same time draw near to God in them.

PART VII.

CONFIDENCE IN GOD IN THE FACE OF DEATH

IT IS a pleasing consideration, that amidst the spiritual darkness which unhappily prevails in many parts of the land, God nevertheless has a people. It not infrequently happens that single individuals are to be found, who, though very disadvantageously situated with regard to the ordinary means of grace, have received truly saving impressions, and through a blessing on secret meditation, reading, and prayer, are led to the closest communion with God, and become eminently devoted Christians. It is no small error of too many professors of the present day, to overlook or undervalue the instances of this kind which exist. The religious profession and opinions of some have too much of mere machinery in their composition. If every wheel, pivot, chain, spring, cog, or pinion, be not exactly in its place, or move not precisely according to a favourite and prescribed system the whole is rejected as unworthy of regard. But happily 'the Lord knoweth them that are His'; nor is the impression of His own seal wanting to characterise some who, in comparative seclusion from the religious world, 'name the name of Christ. and depart from iniquity.'

There are some real Christians so peculiarly circumstanced in this respect, as to illustrate the poet's comparison,

"Full many a gem of purest ray serene
The dark unfathom'd caves of ocean bear;
Full many a flower is born to blush unseen,
And waste its sweetness on the desert air."

Yet this was not altogether the case with the Dairyman's daughter. Her religion had indeed ripened in seclusion from the world, and she was intimately known but to few; but she lived usefully, departed most happily, and left a shining track behind her. While I attempt a faint delineation of it, may I catch its influence, and become, through inexpressible mercy, a follower of 'them who through faith and patience inherit the promises!'

From the time wherein I visited her, as described in my last paper, I considered her end as fast approaching. One day I received a hasty summons to inform me that she was dying. It was brought by a soldier, whose countenance bespoke seriousness, good sense, and piety.

'I am sent. Sir, by the father and mother of Elizabeth W——, at her own particular request, to say how much they all wished to see you. She is going home, Sir, very fast indeed.'

'Have you known her long?'

'About a month, Sir. I love to visit the sick; and hearing of her case from a person who lives close by our camp, I went to see her. I bless God that ever I did go. Her conversation has been very profitable to me.'

'I rejoice,' said I, 'to see in you, as I trust, a brother soldier. Though we differ in our outward regimentals, I hope we serve under the same spiritual Captain. I will go with you.'

My horse was soon ready. My military companion walked by my side, and gratified me with very sensible and pious conversation. He related some remarkable testimonies of the excellent disposition of the Dairyman's daughter, as they appeared from recent intercourse which he had had with her.

'She is a bright diamond, Sir,' said the soldier, 'and will soon shine brighter than any diamond upon earth.'

We passed through lanes and fields, over hills and valleys, by open and retired paths, sometimes crossing over, and sometimes following the windings of a little brook, which gently murmured by the roadside. Conversation beguiled the distance, and shortened the apparent time of our journey, till we were nearly arrived at the Dairyman's cottage.

As we approached it, we became silent. Thoughts of death, eternity, and salvation, inspired by the sight of a house where a dying believer lay, filled my own mind, and, I doubt not, that of my companion also.

No living object yet appeared, except the Dairyman's dog, keeping a kind of mute watch at the door; for he did not, as formerly, bark at my approach. He seemed to partake so far of the feelings appropriate to the circumstances of the family, as not to wish to give a hasty or painful alarm. He came forward to the little wicket-gate, then looked back at the house door, as if conscious there was sorrow within. It was as if he wanted to say, 'Tread softly over the threshold, as you enter the house of mourning; for my master's heart is full of grief.'

The soldier took my horse and tied it up in a shed. A solemn serenity appeared to surround the whole place: it was only interrupted by the breezes passing through the large elm-trees which stood near the house, and which my imagination indulged itself in thinking were plaintive sighs of sorrow. I gently opened the door; no one appeared, and all was still and silent. The soldier followed; we came to the foot of the stairs.

'They are come,' said a voice, which I knew to be the father's; 'they are come.'

He appeared at the top; I gave him my hand, and said nothing. On entering the room above, I saw the aged mother and her son supporting the much-loved daughter and sister: the son's wife sat weeping in a window-seat, with a child on her lap; two or three persons attended in the room to discharge any office which friendship or necessity might require.

I sat down by the bedside. The mother could not weep, but now and then sighed deeply, as she alternately looked at Elizabeth and at me. The big tear rolled down the brother's cheek, and testified an affectionate regard. The good old man stood at the foot of the bed, leaning upon the post, and unable to take his eyes off the child from whom he was so soon to part.

Elizabeth's eyes were closed, and as yet she perceived me not. But over the face, though pale, sunk, and hollow, the peace of God, which passeth all understanding, had cast a triumphant calm.

The soldier, after a short pause silently reached out his Bible towards me, pointing with his finger at 1 Cor. xv. 55, 56, 57. I then broke silence by reading the passage, 'Oh death, where is thy sting? O grave, where is thy victory? The sting of death is sin; and the strength of sin is the law. But thanks be to God, which giveth us the victory through our Lord Jesus Christ.'

At the sound of these words her eyes opened, and something like a ray of divine light beamed on her countenance, as she said. 'Victory! victory! through our Lord Jesus Christ.'

She relapsed again, taking no further notice of anyone present.

'God be praised for the triumph of faith!' said I.

'Amen,' replied the soldier.

The Dairyman's uplifted eye showed that the Amen was in his heart, though his tongue failed to utter it.

A short struggling for breath took place in the dying young woman, which was soon over; and then I said to her:

'My dear friend, do you not feel that you are supported?

'The Lord deals very gently with me.' she replied.

'Are not His promises now very precious to you?'

'They are all yea and amen in Christ Jesus.'

'Are you in much bodily pain?'

'So little that I almost forget it.'

'How good the Lord is!'

'And how unworthy am I!'

'You are going to see Him as He is.'

'I think—I hope—I believe that I am.' She again fell into a short slumber.

Looking at her mother, I said, 'What a mercy to have a child so near heaven as yours is!'

'And what a mercy.' she replied, in broken accents, 'if her I poor old mother might but follow her there! But, Sir, it is so hard to part.'

'I hope through grace by faith you will soon meet to part no more; it will be but a little while.'

'Sir,' said the Dairyman, 'that thought supports me, and the Lord's goodness makes me feel more reconciled than I was.'

'Father——mother——,' said the reviving daughter, 'He is good to me—trust Him, praise Him evermore.'

'Sir,' added she, in a faint voice, 'I want to thank you for your kindness to me——I want to ask a favour; ——you buried my sister——will you do the same for me?'

'All shall be as you wish, if God permit,' I replied.

'Thank you, Sir, thank you;——I have another favour to ask.——When I am gone, remember my father and mother. They are old, but I hope the good work is begun in their souls——My prayers are heard——Pray come and see them.——I cannot speak much, but I want to speak for their sakes——Sir, remember them.'

The aged parents now sighed and sobbed aloud, uttering broken sentences, and gained some relief by such an expression of their feelings.

At length I said to Elizabeth, 'Do you experience any doubts or temptations on the subject of your eternal safety?'

'No, Sir. The Lord deals very gently with me, and gives me peace.'

'What are your views of the dark valley of death, now that you are passing through it?'

'It is *not* dark.'

'Why so?'

'My Lord is *there*, and He is my light and my salvation.'

'Have you any fears of more bodily suffering?'

'The Lord deals so gently with me, I can trust Him.'

Something of a convulsion came on. When it was past, she said again and again,

'The Lord deals very gently with me. Lord, I am Thine; save me.——Blessed Jesus——precious Saviour ——His blood cleanseth from all sin——Who shall separate?——His name is Wonderful——Thanks be to God——He giveth the victory——I, even I, am saved ——O grace, mercy, and wonder!——Lord, receive my spirit!——Dear Sir,——dear father, mother, friends, I am going——but all is well, well, well——.'

She relapsed again. —We knelt down to prayer. — The Lord was in the midst of us, and blessed us. She did not again revive while I remained, nor ever speak any more words which could be understood. She slumbered for about ten hours, and at last sweetly fell asleep in the arms of that Lord who had dealt so gently with her.

I left the house an hour after she had ceased to speak. I pressed her hand as I was taking leave, and said. 'Christ is the resurrection and the life.' She gently returned the pressure, but could neither open her eyes nor utter a reply.

I never had witnessed a scene so impressive as this before. It completely filled my imagination as I returned home.

'Farewell,' thought I. 'dear friend, till the morning of an eternal day shall renew our personal intercourse. Thou wast a brand plucked from the burning, that thou mightest become a star shining in the firmament of glory. I have seen thy light and thy good works, and will therefore glorify our Father which is in heaven. I have seen in thy example, what it is to be a sinner freely saved by grace. I have learned from thee, as in a living mirror, who it is that begins, continues, and ends the work of faith and love. Jesus is All in all; He will and shall be glorified. He won the crown, and alone deserves to wear it. May no one attempt to rob Him of His glory! He saves, and saves to the uttermost. Farewell, dear sister in the Lord. Thy flesh and thy heart may fall; but God is the strength of thy heart, and shall be thy portion for ever.'

PART VIII.

DEATH INSPIRES SOLEMN THOUGHTS

WHO CAN conceive or estimate the nature of that change which the soul of a believer must experience at the moment when, quitting its tabernacle of clay, it suddenly enters into the presence of God? If, even while 'we see through a glass darkly,' the views of divine love and wisdom are so delightful to the eye of faith; what must be the glorious vision of God, when seen face to face! If it be so valued a privilege here on earth to enjoy the communion of saints, and to take sweet counsel together with our fellow-travellers towards the heavenly kingdom; what shall we see and know when we finally 'come unto Mount Zion, and unto the city of the living God, the heavenly Jerusalem, and to an innumerable company of angels, to the general assembly and church of the first-born, which are written in heaven, and to God the Judge of all, and to the spirits of just men made perfect, and to Jesus the mediator of the new covenant'?

If, during the sighs and tears of a mortal pilgrimage, the consolations of the Spirit are so precious, and the hope full of immortality is so animating to the soul; what heart can conceive, or what tongue utter its superior joys, when arrived at the state where sighing and sorrow flee away, and the tears shall be wiped from every eye?

Such ideas were powerfully associated together in my imagination, as I travelled onward to the house where, in solemn preparation for the grave, lay the remains of the Dairyman's daughter.

She had breathed her last shortly after the visit related in my former account. Permission was obtained, as before in the case of her sister, that I should perform the funeral service. Many pleasing yet melancholy thoughts were connected with the fulfilment of this task. I retraced the numerous and important conversations which I had held with her. But these could now no longer be maintained on earth. I reflected on the interesting and improving nature of Christian friendships, whether formed in palaces or in cottages; and felt thankful that I had so long enjoyed that privilege with the subject of this memorial. I then indulged a selfish sigh for a moment, on thinking that I could no longer hear the great truths of Christianity uttered by one who had drunk so deep of the waters of the river of life. But the rising murmur was checked by the animating thought. 'she is gone to eternal rest—could I wish her back again in this vale of tears?'

At that moment the first sound of a tolling bell struck my ear. It proceeded from a village church in the valley directly beneath the ridge of a high hill, over which I had taken my way. It was Elizabeth's funeral knell.

The sound was solemn; and in ascending to the elevated spot over which I rode, it acquired a peculiar tone and character. Tolling at slow and regular intervals (as was customary for a considerable time previous to the hour of burial), the bell, as it were, proclaimed the blessedness of the dead who die in the Lord, and also the necessity of the living pondering these things, and laying them to heart. It seemed to say, 'Hear my warning voice, thou son of man. There is but a step between thee and death. Arise, prepare thine house; for thou shalt die, and not live.'

The scenery was in unison with that tranquil frame of mind which is most suitable for holy meditation. A rich and fruitful valley lay immediately beneath; it was adorned with cornfields and pastures, through which a small river winded in a variety of directions, and many herds grazed upon its banks. A fine range of opposite hills, covered with grazing flocks, terminated with a bold sweep into the ocean, whose blue waves appeared at a distance beyond. Several villages, hamlets, and churches, were scattered in the valley. The noble mansions of the rich, and the lowly cottages of the poor, added their respective features to the landscape. The air was mild, and the declining sun occasioned a beautiful interchange of light and shade upon the sides of the hills. In the midst of this scene, the chief sound that arrested attention was the bell tolling for the funeral of the Dairyman's daughter.

Do any of my readers inquire why I describe so minutely the circumstances of prospect and scenery which may be connected with the incidents I relate? My reply is, that the God of redemption is the God of creation likewise; and that we are taught in every part of the Word of God to unite the admiration of the beauties and wonders of nature to every other motive for devotion. When David considered the heavens, the work of God's fingers, the moon and the stars which He has ordained, he was thereby led to the deepest humiliation of heart before his Maker. And when he viewed the sheep and the oxen and the beasts of the field. the fowls of the air and the fish of the sea, he was constrained to cry out, 'O Lord, our Lord, how excellent is Thy name in all the earth!'

I am the poor man's friend, and wish more especially that every poor labouring man should know how to connect the goodness of God in creation and providence with the unsearchable riches of his grace in the salvation of a sinner. And where can he learn this lesson more instructively than in looking around the fields where his labour is appointed, and there tracing the handiwork of

God in all that he beholds? Such meditations have often afforded me both profit and pleasure, and I wish my readers to share them with me.

The Dairyman's cottage was rather more than a mile distant from the church. A lane, quite overshaded with trees and high hedges, led from the foot of the hill to his dwelling. It was impossible at that time to overlook the suitable gloom of such an approach to the house of mourning.

I found, on my entrance, that several Christian friends, from different parts of the neighbourhood, had assembled together, to pay their last tribute of esteem and regard to the memory of the Dairyman's daughter. Several of them had first become acquainted with her during the latter stage of her illness: some few had maintained an affectionate intercourse with her for a longer period. But all seemed anxious to manifest their respect for one who was endeared to them by such striking testimonies of true Christianity.

I was requested to go into the chamber where the relatives and a few other friends were gone to take a last look at the remains of Elizabeth.

It is not easy to describe the sensation which the mind experiences on the first sight of a dead countenance, which, when living, was loving and esteemed for the sake of that soul which used to give it animation. A deep and awful view of the separation that has taken place between the soul and body of the deceased, since we last beheld them, occupies the feelings; our friend seems to be both near, and yet far off. The most interesting and valuable part is fled away; what remains is but the earthly, perishing habitation, no longer occupied by its tenant. Yet the features present the accustomed association of friendly intercourse. For one moment, we could think them asleep. The next reminds us that the blood circulates no more; the eye has lost its power of seeing, the ear of hearing, the heart of throbbing, and the limbs of moving. Quickly a thought of glory breaks in upon the mind, and we imagine the dear departed soul to be arrived at its long-wished for rest. It is surrounded by cherubim and seraphim, and sings the song of Moses and the Lamb on Mount Zion. Amid the solemn stillness of the chamber of death, imagination hears heavenly hymns chanted by the spirits of just men made perfect. In another moment, the livid lips and sunken eye of the clay-cold corpse recall our thoughts to earth, and to ourselves again. And while we think of mortality, sin, death, and the grave, we feel the prayer rise in our bosom, 'Let me die the death of the righteous, and let my last end be like his.'

If there be a moment when Christ and salvation, death, judgment, heaven, and hell, appear more than ever to be momentous subjects of meditation, it is that which brings us to the side of a coffin containing the body of a departed believer.

Elizabeth's features were altered, but much of her likeness remained. Her father and mother sat at the head, her brother at the foot, of the coffin. The father silently and alternately looked upon his dead child and then lifted up his eyes to heaven. A struggle for resignation to the will of God was manifest in his countenance; while the tears rolling down his aged cheeks, at the same time declared his grief and affection. The poor mother cried and sobbed aloud, and appeared to be much overcome by the shock of separation from a daughter so justly dear to her. The weakness and infirmity of old age added a character to her sorrow, which called for much tenderness and compassion.

A remarkably decent-looking woman who had the management of the few simple, though solemn ceremonies which the case required, advanced towards me, saying,

'Sir, this is rather a sight of joy than of sorrow. Our dear friend Elizabeth finds it to be so, I have no doubt. She is beyond all sorrow: do you not think she is, Sir?'

'After what I have known, and seen and heard,' I replied, 'I feel the fullest assurance, that while her body remains here, her soul is with her Saviour in paradise. She loved Him *here*, and *there* she enjoys the pleasures which are at His right hand for evermore.'

'Mercy, mercy upon a poor old creature almost broken down with age and grief!—What shall I do!—Betsy's gone. My daughter's dead.—O my child! I shall never see thee more.—God be merciful to me a sinner!' sobbed out the poor mother.

'That last prayer, my dear good woman,' said I, 'will bring you and your child together again. It is a cry that has brought thousands to glory. It brought your daughter there, and I hope it will bring you thither likewise. God will in no wise cast out any that come to Him.'

'My dear,' said the Dairyman, breaking the long silence he had maintained, 'let us trust God with our child; and let us trust Him with our own selves. The Lord gave, and the Lord has taken away; blessed be the name of the Lord! We are old, and can have but a little further to travel in our journey, and then—' he could say no more.

The soldier, mentioned in my last paper, reached a Bible into my hand, and said, 'Perhaps, Sir, you would not object to reading a chapter before we go to the church?'

I did so; it was the fourteenth of the book of Job. A sweet tranquility prevailed while I read it. Each minute that was spent in this funeral chamber seemed to be valuable. I made a few observations on the chapter, and connected them with the case of our departed sister.

'I am but a poor soldier,' said our military friend, 'and have nothing of this world's goods beyond my daily subsistence; but I would not exchange my hope of salvation in the next world for all that this world could bestow without it. What is wealth without grace? Blessed be God, as I march about from one quarter to another, I still find the Lord wherever I go; and, thanks be to His holy Name, He is here to-day in the midst of this company of the living and the dead. I feel that it is good to be here.'

Some other persons present began to take a part in our conversation, in the course of which the life and experience of the Dairyman's daughter were brought forward in a very interesting manner. Each friend had something to relate in testimony of her gracious disposition. A young woman under twenty, who had hitherto been a very light and trifling character, appeared to be remarkably impressed by the conversation of that day; and I have since had ground to believe that divine grace then began to influence her in the choice of that better part which shall not be taken from her.

What a contrast does such a scene as this exhibit, when compared with the dull, formal, unedifying, and often indecent manner, in which funeral parties assemble in the house of death!

As we conversed, the parents revived. Our subject of discourse was delightful to their hearts. Their child seemed almost to be alive again, while we talked of her. Tearful smiles often brightened their countenances, as they heard the voice of friendship uttering their daughter's praises; or rather the praises of Him who had made her a vessel of mercy, and an instrument of spiritual good to her family.

The time for departing to the church was now at hand.

I went to take my last look at the deceased.

There was much written on her countenance. She had evidently died with a smile. It still remained, and spoke the tranquility of her departed soul. According to the custom of the country, she was decorated with leaves and flowers in the coffin; she seemed as a bride gone forth to meet the Bridegroom. These, indeed, were fading flowers, but they reminded me of that paradise whose flowers are immortal, and where her never-dying soul is at rest.

I remembered the last words which I had heard her speak, and was instantly struck with the happy thought, that 'death was indeed swallowed up in victory.'

As I slowly retired, I said inwardly, 'Peace, my honoured sister, be to *thy* memory and to *my* soul, till we meet in the better world.'

In a little time the procession formed: it was rendered the more interesting by the consideration of so many that followed the coffin being persons of a devout and spiritual character. The distance was rather more than a mile. I resolved to continue with and go before them, as they moved slowly onwards.

Immediately after the body came the venerable father and mother,[1] bending with age, and weeping through much affliction of heart. Their appearance was calculated to excite every emotion of pity, love, and esteem. The other relatives followed them in order, and the several attendant friends took their places behind.

After we had advanced about a hundred yards, my meditation was unexpectedly and most agreeably

---

[1] The mother died not long after her daughter; and I have good reason to believe that God was merciful to her, and took her to Himself.

An interesting account of a visit recently made to the Dairyman's cottage appeared in the Christian Guardian for October 1813. A still more recent visit to the good old Dairyman (who still lives, at the age of 82) has been made by the author of this narrative (June 1814).

The good old Dairyman died in 1816. His end was eminently Christian.

interrupted by the friends who attended beginning to sing a funeral psalm. Nothing could be more sweet or solemn. The well-known effect of the open air in softening and blending the sounds of music, was here peculiarly felt. The road through which we passed was beautiful and romantic. It lay at the foot of a hill, which occasionally re-echoed the voices of the singers, and seemed to give faint replies to the notes of the mourners. The funeral knell was distinctly heard from the church tower, and greatly increased the effect which this simple and becoming service produced.

We went by several cottages: a respectful attention was universally observed as we passed; and the countenances of many proclaimed their regard for the departed young woman. The singing was regularly continued, with occasional intervals of about five minutes, during our whole progress.

I cannot describe the state of my own mind as peculiarly connected with this solemn singing. I was reminded of older times and ancient piety. I wished the practice more frequent. It seems well calculated to excite and cherish devotion and religious affections.

Music, when judiciously brought into the service of religion, is one of the most delightful, and not least efficacious, means of grace. I pretend not too minutely to conjecture as to the actual nature of those pleasures which, after the resurrection. the reunited body and soul will enjoy in heaven; but I can hardly persuade myself that melody and harmony will be wanting, when even the sense of hearing shall itself be glorified.

We at length arrived at the church. Looking upwards, as I drew near the church, I observed a dial on the wall. The sun's declining rays directed the shadow to the evening hour. As I passed underneath this simple but solemn monitor, I was reminded of the lapse of time, the uncertainty of life, and sure approach of eternity. I thought with David, 'We are strangers before Thee, and sojourners, as were all our fathers; our days on earth are as a shadow, and there is none abiding.' 'Lord, so teach us to number our days, that we may apply our hearts unto wisdom.'

The service was heard with deep and affectionate attention. When we came to the grave, the hymn which Elizabeth had selected was sung. All was devout, simple, animating. We committed our dear sister's body to the earth, in full hope of a joyful resurrection from the dead.

Thus was the veil of separation drawn for a season. She is departed, and no more seen. But she will be seen on the right hand of her Redeemer at the last day; and will again appear to His glory, a miracle of grace and monument of mercy.

My reader, rich or poor, shall you and I appear there likewise? Are we 'clothed with humility,' and arrayed in the wedding garment of a Redeemer's righteousness? Are we turned from idols to serve the living God? Are we sensible of our own emptiness, and therefore flying to a Saviour's fulness to obtain grace and strength? Do we indeed live in Christ and on Him and by Him, and with Him? Is He our All in all? Are we 'lost, and found?' 'dead, and alive again?'

My *poor* reader, the Dairyman's daughter was a *poor* girl, and the child of a *poor* man. Herein thou resemblest *her*, but dost thou resemble her, as she resembled Christ? Art thou made rich by faith? Hast thou a crown laid up for thee? Is thine heart set upon heavenly riches? If not, read this story once more, and then pray earnestly for like precious faith.

But if, through grace, thou dost love and serve the Redeemer that saved the Dairyman's daughter, grace, Peace, and mercy be with thee! The lines are fallen unto thee in pleasant places: thou hast a goodly heritage. Press forward in duty, and wait upon the Lord, possessing thy soul in holy patience. Thou hast just been with me to the grave of a departed believer. Now 'go thy way till the end be; for thou shalt rest, and stand in thy lot at the end of the days.'

APPENDIX

THE FIRST two letters were addressed by the Dairyman's daughter to her father. I of course omit those passages which are strictly personal and private.

LETTER I

To MR JOSEPH WALLBRIDGE.
Southampton, Feb. 23.1797.

My DEAR AND HONOURED FATHER,

.   .   .   .

And now. my dear father. I do not know what to say to change the scene. I suppose you were a little alarmed the other day, when the fleet of colliers came in, and they were taken for French. It was reported here that they were landed at several places; and we should have soon been over in the island for shelter from them; as if by that means we could 'flee from the wrath to come,' or stay the hand of an almighty and justly avenging God, Who, for the sins of mankind, has sent His judgments abroad in the earth. And even now we are ready to say to that God Who hath so long withheld the sword of vengeance from destroying us, and still extends His everlasting arms of mercy to save us. 'Depart from us'—for we desire not the knowledge of Him. But I hope, my dear father, that the Lord will have mercy on us, and bring us out of that gross darkness into His marvellous light, and set our feet on that Rock that is higher than we are. But we are informed by the Word of God. that if we would have all these blessings bestowed on us, we must fix all our hopes and our faith on the blessed Lamb of God that was slain to redeem the fallen children of Adam. For 'as in Adam all die, so shall all' true believers 'in Christ be made alive' to God: and then, my dear father, we may say—

> 'Prisoners of hope, lift up your heads,
> The day of liberty draws near;
> Jesus, Who on the serpent treads,
> Shall soon in your behalf appear:
> The Lord will to His temple come,
> Prepare your hearts to make Him room.'

My dear father, I hope that God will not suffer sickness or death ever to surprise us unawares, or find us in a state unprepared.

.   .   .   .

Please give my duty to my dear and tender mother, and accept the same yourself, and love to dear brothers and sisters; and may the blessed Spirit of God be very powerful in all your hearts to root out every evil!

LETTER II

Southampton, April 11. 1797.

My DEAR FATHER,

I have been silent longer than I should, had my dear sister written before; but as I know all things are guided and governed by Him Whom my soul loveth, I wait patiently His appointed time. O my dear father, it is good to trust in Him, to call upon Him, to honour His holy name. Oh, if you have not tasted how good and gracious the Lord is, then turn and seek Him while He may be found; None ever sought His glorious face in vain; and those 'that come unto Me' (saith the dear Lamb of God) 'I will in no wise cast out.' No: His tender love, pity, and compassion never fall to poor sinners. No: though my dear mother and father have lived to near the time that my God hath said shall be the age of man, and ye have still been sinning and grieving, and hiding, as it were, your faces from that God Who is still pursuing you with His love and mercy, yea, even the blessed Jesus, Who is still making intercession for sinners at His Father's right hand.

> 'When Justice bared the sword
>   To cut the fig-tree down,
> The pity of my Lord
>   Cried, Let it still alone: The
> Father mild inclined His ear,
>   And spared us yet another year.'

But remember, my dear friends, His blessed words: 'My Spirit shall not always strive with man': and 'Except ye are born again, ye cannot inherit the kingdom of heaven'; and if you are not washed in the precious blood of that dear Lamb of God, you can have no part with Him; and if His Spirit does not 'bear witness with your spirit' that you are born of God, you are still in your sins, and strangers to the blood that bought you on the tree. Oh! my daily prayer to God is, that He will 'turn you, and so shall you be turned.' Oh! the dear Redeemer still waits to be gracious; He is ever ready to pardon your sins, and seal it with His precious blood; He is ever calling, 'Come unto Me, all ye that labour and are heavy laden' with the burden of your sins, 'and I will give you rest.' Then I entreat you, my dear friends, in the name of the Most High God, that ye turn and lay hold of the ever-blessed Jesus as

91

your shield of faith, and He will arm you with the whole armour of God. But remember this: though God is full of love and mercy, yet He will be sought unto. Then draw nigh unto God in secret prayer, and God will draw nigh unto your precious souls, and that to bless them; and will say unto you, Believe on Me, 'My grace is sufficient for you,' I will cleanse you in My precious blood; and then shall your leprosy be healed, and you shall return without spot. And then you must watch and pray to Him continually to keep you clean. Oh, He is always more ready to hear than we are to pray, and more ready to give than we to ask! Remember, my dear father, that the language of every prayerless and unconverted soul is, 'Depart from me, O God; for we desire not the knowledge of the Most High.' Then put off the evil day no longer, lest you should hear Him say, Who is willing and able to save to the uttermost those that come unto Him, 'I have stretched out My hand all the day long, and no man regarded.' And, 'Behold. I knock at the door of every man's heart, and to him that openeth unto Me. I will come in and sup with him, and he with Me.' My dear father, those are blessed and comfortable words: and I am His living witness, and I 'set to my seal' that Jesus is true. Oh, the happy state of the children of God! Now I ask and receive; I seek and I find Him Whom my soul loveth; yea. I always find I have a very near access, through His blessed intercession, to supplicate the throne of grace; and now I can say—

> 'Before the throne my Surety stands.
> My name is written on His hands';

and now I am so filled up with the peace and love of God, that I can lift up my soul and say,

> 'My God, I know, I feel Thee mine,

And will not quit my claim,
Till all I have is lost in Thine,
And all renewed I am';

and,

'Where'er I am, where'er I move,
I meet the object of my love.'

The Lord doth so strengthen my faith in Him, that I find all His promises stand engaged to make me blessed. Oh, may God pardon what this poor unworthy dust has written, through ignorance, which is not agreeable to His most blessed will, which I will ever seek to fulfil!

.   .   .   .

I have so little taste for the conversation of this world, that it is very unpleasant to think on it. My sister's love and duty to all. Mrs. B. will be in the island soon. please God, and then you are to write to her. Desire my brother to write too, and direct her to the house of God in Bath, for she is still walking in darkness, and is ignorant of it. Oh may the Lord be graciously pleased to bring you all into His marvellous light, that you may praise Him in time and eternity: then strive to enter in at the strait gate. ... If the Lord shall please to spare me, I hope to see you ere long; if not in this world. in that where we shall bask in unutterable bliss. My dear friends, take not this advice amiss from your unworthy child: it is the command of my blessed Lord. 'When thou art converted, remember thy brethren': and I daily take up my cross and follow Him whithersoever He goeth; and I pray God enable you to do the same. Oh, how should I rejoice and praise my God to see you enabled through the inspiration of the Spirit of the Most High, to answer this ill-written letter! —Farewell, in the Lord. dear friends.

The third letter is to her sister.

LETTER III

Cowes. October 14, 1798.

My DEAR SISTER,

I have not had a convenient opportunity to write till now. I hope you have not been unhappy at my long silence. Consider that God is my keeper, therefore I shall lack no manner of thing that is good. I entreat you to commend the keeping of your soul, spirit, and body, to the Lord, for He is a promise-making, and a true and faithful promise-keeping God.

'Then let me commend my Saviour to you,
The publican's friend and advocate too.'

My dear, I say that God is my keeper: you will say He is yours; it is true, for 'in Him we all live, and move, and have our being'; but I can say with Job. 'I know that my Redeemer liveth'; and 'He is now pleading His merits and death. And still interceding for sinners beneath: and He is waiting to be gracious to you for He is long-suffering and kind, plenteous in goodness; His love and mercy know no end or bounds, and His compassions fall not: now, my dear,

'Ready to you the angels wait,
To triumph in your blest estate:
Tuning their harps. they long to praise
The wonders of redeeming grace.'

O my dear sister, search the Scriptures diligently; pray to God earnestly; for, in so doing, you will find that

He is a God 'nigh at hand, and not afar off.' He has promised to be found of those that seek Him; for none ever sought His face in vain, neither did ever any trust in Him and was deceived. O my dear sister, if you did but believe, how willing God is to reveal His Son in your heart, the hope of glory! Oh, how would your soul be ravished, if Christ would appear to you the altogether lovely, and the first among ten thousand! Then could you say those blessed words—

'My soul, through my Redeemer's love,
Saved from the second death I feel;
My eyes from tears of dark despair,
My feet from falling into hell.

'Wherefore my feet to Him shall run,
My eyes on His perfections gaze,
My soul shall live for God alone,
And all within me shout His praise.'

I entreat you to read the word of God carefully, for in it is eternal life. All the promises there stand engaged to make you blessed, if you truly repent, and forsake your sins, and turn to God with full purpose of heart, and fully believe on the Lord Jesus Christ, and He will save you from your sins with a present and everlasting salvation: for He says, 'Only believe, and thou shalt be saved.' We should receive the Word of God, as if it was the awful voice of God from heaven. It will be awful to the wicked and unconverted. ...Oh, may the Lord quicken your dead soul

'with life divine,
And make you in His image shine!'

Oh, may you feel the kindlings of love divine shed abroad in your heart! Farewell in the Lord, my dear sister.

The following little narrative seems to have been intended for her own private use. It is apparently left unfinished.

November 30. 1800.

ELIZABETH WALLBRIDGE, BORN JULY 29, 1770.

I feel my mind more composed when writing, and more free from wandering thoughts, than at any other time; for I have little retirement, and when I have, it is seldom free from disturbances, so that I am almost continually conversant with the world. The Lord knoweth what a burden it is to my mind, and how impatient I have been. May the Lord pardon His unfaithful, unprofitable servant, and sanctify me throughout, Soul, spirit, and body, and plunge me in the Godhead's deepest sea, that I may be lost in His immensity! Oh, glorious hope of perfect love! May it ever fill and lift my ravished spirit up to things above. There I shall for ever love.

I thought I would just set down, as the Lord is pleased to give me time and strength, a few of His particular mercies and favours as I can recollect. He has abounded in love and mercy to me: oh, that I had made Him all the returns that love can make, by giving myself a sacrifice daily unto Him! But now I have to lament my shortcomings, and to apply to the 'blood of sprinkling.' which speaks my sins forgiven, and purifies my soul, and makes it meet for heaven. Oh, what a precious Saviour have I found! Oh, that I could make Him known to all mankind, that all may turn and taste the riches of His grace! At present I am so very weak in body and mind, that I can recollect but very little: it has been decaying near four years; but in the Lord Jehovah is my everlasting strength, and whoever relies on Him shall never be ashamed, and shall be freed from all slavish fears.

I seemed to have some fear of God, and love to Him, from my childhood. His restraining grace kept me from falling into great and open sin, and gave me such a love to truth and uprightness, that I seemed to hate every false way, word, and work in myself and others. I remember, when I went to school, one of my playmates that I was very fond of used to take every opportunity to get money from her mother unknown to her, and bring to school, and buy all kinds of toys, and then freely give me and another or two an equal share herself. But Oh, how did the Spirit of the Lord strive with me at that time, and convince me of the evil, so that I had no peace of mind whilst I partook of the sin, and yet I had not strength to resist it! It was so on my mind that I ought to make her fault known, not to conceal it and partake of part. I could see it a great evil in the person that sold her the things, whose daughter took part, and, I believe, knew as well as I did how she came by it; but I never revealed it, though I always bore it on my mind with abhorrence. What a sad thing to yield to sin, against such clear convictions!

I was early taught a form of prayer, which I continued to repeat in a careless manner when I was laid down in bed, but very often I fell asleep before I said them half. But, blessed be God. He still spared me, and often drew me to Himself by the cords of love: for at an early age He drew me to secret prayer, where I often felt the kindlings of His love; but had none to set me forward, so that I often neglected this duty; but when alone, I have often felt great sweetness in it. I believe if I had heard the gospel preached I should have been very devoted to that God I now love and adore. But I do not yet love Him, as

He has promised I shall, with all my loving heart, when sin is all destroyed. O happy moment, how I long for it!

The last document is

HER WILL

My dear father, and mother, and brothers—if it should please the Lord to spare you all till after my decease, I take this opportunity to set down what I simply desire, if it be the Lord's will, and agreeable to you all. If I die under this roof, it will be best, as soon as I am dead. to have my coffin made; let Mr —— make it, if it is quite agreeable: and then I can be carried downstairs, not to disturb you or break your rest. And there the angels of my covenant-making and promise-keeping God will watch over me and protect my sleeping dust; so that you need not fear any evil spirit, for they will have done with me for ever; they will never assault me any more. I shall then, through Christ, Who hath loved me with an everlasting love, gain the glorious victory over all the principalities and powers of darkness; for they know that I am a redeemed captive from their power, though they cease not to tempt me to return to my former customs, that I may be again in bondage to fear: but glory be given to God, His grace is sufficient for me; hitherto He hath brought me safe through, and I know He will save to the end. May I lift up my heart to Him and cry—O thou
'Fairer than the sons of men.
Do not let me turn again!'

Let my coffin be very plain, neat and strong, made to cover very close. Let it be made white inside and out, if no trouble; and for my shroud a little wool will do, if you like it: it will be less expense; for it will all turn to dust. I care not whom you ask to my funeral; I want no form of young people. I had rather have those that love God, that they may rejoice over me with angels above, and praise a God of love. (*She then names several friends whom she desired to be present. and proceeds.*) Let them all meet together that can or will come ... and I trust they will feel the Lord powerfully present in the midst to bless every waiting soul, and reveal the secrets of His love. Mr Richmond, or the minister of Newchurch, which you please; I love them both, because they love God: for 'God is love.' and His love constrains us to love one another. ... Do not be afraid of disturbing the peaceful dead in singing praises to God and the Lamb Who hath redeemed me from sin. It may be, my happy spirit may be permitted to join with listening angels who catch the approving sound, while all heaven's host cry—A child is born into our world above.

Let these hymns be sung: the 37th, 'Hosanna to Jesus on high'; the 38th, ''Tis finished, 'tis done'; the 23rd, 'Ah, lovely appearance of death'; the 50th, in the large book. 'Hark, a voice divides the sky.' If the preacher please, for the glory of God, and the good of the living, let him preach a sermon from Psalm cxvi. 15,—'Precious in the sight of the Lord is the death of His saints'; and may the Word be attended with power; a divine energy and the quickening influence of the Spirit of God rest upon the ministers and the hearers, that glory may be given to God, and great good done in His precious name; that His saints who love Him may be strengthened and refreshed and built up in their most holy faith; that they may go on their way rejoicing in the strength of the Lord, from grace to grace, till glory end what grace began; that they may be fully prepared to meet death with Christian courage. And may all my dear friends follow on to know the Lord, and experimentally to feel the saving power of divine grace in each of their hearts, that they may give glory to God, and triumphantly quit the stage of mortality, shouting victory through the blood of the Lamb, Who now is ascended on high for ever to reign. But I would have all to remember, if they have never yet been convinced of their lost and miserable state by nature, that it is high time for them to awake out of sleep, and cry mightily to God to show them their danger, and save them from destruction. For without faith and prayer you cannot be saved. Then come like the humble publican, with a feeling sense of your sins, and true faith in HIS merits to atone for your sins, and cleanse your guilty souls, and you will be sure to find mercy, pardon, and peace, and grace to help you in every time of need.

When I was brought home, I was in great hopes I should see a great change: but I have been painfully disappointed to the present moment, which often fills my heart with grief and sorrow, to see sinners so unconcerned upon the brink of death. But if I am never permitted to see that happy change, I hope you will experience it, and meet me in glory; there we shall part no more. (*The remainder is occupied with the distribution of her little property, consisting almost entirely of wearing apparel, among her relatives.*)

The following letters, addressed to the Dairyman's daughter by Mr Richmond, are inserted as characteristic illustrations of the style in which he addressed her:—

LETTER I

It has pleased God, my Christian sister, for several weeks past, to keep me in a state of sickness, from which soon, by His goodness, I hope to be relieved. I am at present unable to say half of what I wish to you; but lest you should suspect me of inattention to your friendly and welcome letter. I write these few lines to say, that you shall either hear from me at length, or see me shortly. May God support you through your trial of ill-health; and the nearer you approach the other world, whenever it be God's appointed time, may you be more heavenly-minded!— Peace be multiplied to you. I pray for you, and beg you to know

How faithfully I am
Yours in Christ,
L. RICHMOND.

LETTER II

You may be assured, upon the faith of one who loves God, and would fain serve and obey Him, that you are not out of my mind, though I have been prevented from doing myself the pleasure of calling upon you. I have also delayed writing till now, from an almost daily expectation of coming your way; but as it has happened otherwise, I now acknowledge the receipt of your last letter, and rejoice at the sight of words dictated by a spirit of godliness, humility, and love. In a perverse and adulterous generation, like the present one, what can be so cheering to the soul as converse with those who really know the Lord, and love Him because He hath first loved them? I am well convinced of the propriety and force of your advice with respect to my conduct, and that of the ministers of the gospel in general. God grant such a weak and unprofitable servant as I am, may find grace and ability to conduct myself as becomes a faithful labourer in the vineyard! For who can do it of his own strength? What are the natural powers of sinful man to work out the righteousness of God? To the Spirit of Christ, which changeth and strengtheneth the inner man, we must attribute all: to Him be honour, glory, and praise in all the churches, now and evermore.

I have read your two books, and find much profit in them both. It appears that the life of Madame Guion should be attended to with some caution, which Mr Wesley very frequently draws our observation to in his short notes at the bottom of the pages. She was sometimes influenced by notions which had not sufficiently strong *Scriptural* foundation, and therefore in *these things* should not be as a pattern; but her love of God, and her anxiety to be for ever joined to Him, are lovely and interesting. The rule for discerning the motions and operation of the blessed Spirit within us, is to compare our feelings with those ways of holiness, happy fruits of the Spirit, which the apostle describes: let everything be referred to this as a standard, and we shall never be mistaken. May God so guide and direct you and me to all goodness, that our works may glorify, not *ourselves*—none but Jesus can do that—but our Father which is in heaven. May numbers have reason, through the mercy of God, to bless our memory; and may the seed which in my ministerial capacity I am commissioned to sow, to plant, and to water, receive its due increase from God! I assure you this lies much at my heart, and occupies much of my thoughts: seeing and 'knowing the terrors of the Lord,' I would 'persuade men' with all truth, earnestness, and sincerity, to flee from the wrath to come, and throw themselves and their sins at the foot of the cross, with true repentance and faith. Faith is the hand which we stretch forth to receive the benefits of Christ's blood; it is the soul of the spiritual life, and the grand distinguishing characteristic of the true Christian from the false; it is the touchstone of Christianity; the burning coal which sets fire to the sacrifice on the altar; the sun which enlightens the wilderness of the world; the lantern which guides our feet through the valley of the shadow of death. True faith never can be separated from hope and love; they are three lovely sisters, who take up their dwelling in the heart when it becomes the temple of the Holy Ghost; their parent is God, and their offspring righteous works. How do they shine forth in the midst of a vain and wicked world, like a candle set upon a hill in a dark and gloomy night! May their operations spread wider and wider over the face of the world, and may the Church of God increase in their fruits, till at length the happy time shall arrive when the kingdoms of this world shall become the kingdoms of the Lord and His Anointed. God hasten so blessed a period!

I was much shocked at the sudden death of my neighbour ———. Such unprepared calls ought to operate upon those that are left behind. as salutary warnings. Alive and healthy this morning, who knoweth that this very night our souls shall not be required of us? Let us be on the watch, and endeavour to make others so, for we 'know neither the day nor the hour' of our Master's coming. I am told that his successor has given some strong calls to duty and attentiveness in religion, which I hope in God will prove efficacious. He appears in conversation very much in earnest, and seems steady and persevering; but I have only seen him twice. In that parish you well know how much reformation is wanted. Alas! into what place can we go where it is not wanting? Iniquity triumphs, and presumption darkens the very heavens with her wide-spreading wings; blasphemy, covetousness, and uncleanness, abound and prosper; men are lovers of pleasure, rather than lovers of God. Does not the world go just as Satan would have it? Sometimes he will even suggest to the faithful that their endeavours are in vain, and he tempts to inactivity and sloth; but, blessed be God, the Bible is in our hands, and there we find arguments, and strength, and consolation, and admonition, and precept, and commandment, and encouragement to proceed in the mighty task of beating down the strongholds of iniquity, and destroying the works of the devil. Even though 'the overflowings of ungodliness may make us afraid,' God worketh the good cause, and in the end it shall prosper. The Church shall never fall, nor shall the gates of hell prevail against it.

Your health, I hear, is weak: may God strengthen the inner man, as He thinks fit to weaken the outer; may His kingdom rule in your heart, though the outward fortifications crumble to dust. If it please God to shorten the span of your life, I trust you will meet your Redeemer with peace and joy, and that you will employ the rest of that time which is appointed you on earth, in promoting the cause of righteousness, in combating the artifices of Satan, resisting the ways of ungodliness, conversing with God in fervent prayer and holy meditation, contemplating His redeeming love, and hungering after higher and higher degrees of virtue. May the prospect of a heavenly inheritance keep you alive to holiness and gratitude; and in looking upon the world around, remember that the true spirit of the gospel teaches us to love the sinner whilst we hate sin. Grace, mercy, and peace be multiplied upon you from God and the Lord Jesus Christ.

Believe me to be
Yours, with Christian regard,
L. RICHMOND.